The Haunted House

J. A. GARCIA

Copyright © 2016 J. A. Garcia
All rights reserved
First Edition

PAGE PUBLISHING, INC.
New York, NY

First originally published by Page Publishing, Inc. 2016

ISBN 978-1-68348-659-6 (Paperback)
ISBN 978-1-68348-660-2 (Digital)

Printed in the United States of America

Chapter 1

On a cloudy and gloomy day—the date was September 15, 1986—a group of friends got back from an experience none of them will ever forget. A few days back, the group planned to go on a trip to Universal Studios in California for the very first time. When everyone had all the items and clothes they were going to take on the trip, one of them asked about transportation, because if they were to take their vehicles, it would be pricey, with both the gas fills as well as refills and trouble when they would try to find parking spots close to one another.

A short while later, another one told everyone he had a relative who worked at a vehicle rental place, and might have the vehicle he had in mind for the trip. Then one of the group members asked him what kind of vehicle he had in mind for the trip, and he responded by saying, "A shuttle bus." A moment later, the group agreed that using a shuttle bus for their trip was ideal, and the man quickly went to his vehicle and told them he was going to see his relative right away so as to speed up the process of leaving Mesquite to get on the road toward California.

A few hours later, the man came back driving a shuttle bus, and when he got out of the vehicle, one of them asked what had happened when he talked to his relative at the rental place. He told her his relative gave him the shuttle bus and left his car as collateral in case something happens in or outside the shuttle bus.

The group thought that was a great idea and then went to their houses to get their luggage and lock everything that had to be locked by the time they got to it. When they got back to the shuttle bus to load their luggage in the trunk, all of them entered the bus and seated themselves in wherever they wanted to put themselves.

A moment later, they were all set, and quickly started their way to enter the highway that goes to California. When they got on the highway, everyone got comfortable for the long trip to California. Some rested while the others took out items that would keep them occupied for the trip to Universal Studios, like books, word puzzles, and crossword puzzles.

All of a sudden, it began to rain, and when they passed through the Las Vegas highway, it rained more fiercely. A short while later, after it stopped raining, a tire popped, and the driver slowly went to the side of the road to check and see what tire had popped. After the driver had the bus on the side of the road as well as coming to a complete stop, he parked the bus and went outside to see what tire was out.

A short moment later, the driver came inside through his door and told them the last tire on the left side of the bus was out and he needed help with putting the extra tire on. Three of them went outside with the driver to help put on the extra tire that was below the trunk. One of them went to the trunk to get the jack while the rest went to get the extra tire from the below the trunk.

After, the man got the jack and set it up around where the flat tire was and carefully positioned the bus at an angle where it wouldn't turn over more to the side of the road than it already was. When he got the bus in the perfect angle, he went to see how the others were doing with getting the extra tire, and saw that they were barely getting the tire out of the braces holding it under the trunk.

Once they got the tire out, one of them got the wrench to remove the flat tire and put on the extra tire. A moment later, when they took out the flat tire, all of them noticed something odd between the two tires. One of them said that the flat tire was seventeen inches while the other was fifteen inches, and thought it would complicate things.

THE HAUNTED HOUSE

Everyone agreed the difference in the size of the tire can complicate things, and they thought of any way to resolve it.

One of them came up with an idea, and told everyone his idea. He told them they could still move the bus, but instead of driving, all of them could push it to the nearest gas stop on the road ahead. Everyone thought that was a good idea and agreed to go through with his plan of action to resolve the situation they were in.

A short while later, when they finally got the extra tire in, one of them carefully loosened the jack and put it back in the trunk, where he could take it out from the side of the bus. The driver went to his door and went inside to ask if one of the people still in the bus could put the vehicle in drive as well as steer it. After one of them responded they would do it, the driver went to the back of the bus where the others were positioning themselves in places where they could push the shuttle bus.

When the driver positioned himself in the middle, he told everyone to begin pushing the bus with all their might. A while later, the person at the driver's seat saw something ahead on the road and told everyone what she saw, even the people outside pushing the bus. By the time all of them saw what had she noticed that seemed to be a few yards ahead on the road, everyone who was pushing the bus put in all the strength and force they still had in them.

A few hours later, the group finally got to the thing they all saw. It turned out to be a gas station, which everyone was glad it turned out to be just that. When they got to the gas station and parked the bus, the people pushing the vehicle immediately relaxed and tried to catch their breaths. A moment later, the lady who was in the driver's seat went to the entrance of the gas station to see if anyone could help them.

Then after the lady was at the entrance, she saw it was completely dark inside and the doors were locked. The lady went back to the group to tell them of what she found out about the gas station, and wanted to know what they should do next. A moment later, one of the others in the bus saw what appeared to be a house more ahead on the road.

She then told the group of what she saw ahead on the road. When the group saw the house she told them about, they thought it did seem to be a house to them as well. After everyone saw the house ahead on the road, they agreed to push the bus to the house and see if the owner would let them stay at their house until the weather got better, because it still seemed it could rain, and for quite some time.

A short while later, the group finally got to the house all of them saw but were surprised to see it was surrounded by a metal fence and a somewhat tall gate. When everyone left the bus in the front of the gateway, they quickly went through the gate and to the front door to the house, which turned out to be one that can be compared to a rich person's mansion.

After the group got to the front door of the house, one of them knocked on the door. A moment later, a woman, whom everyone noticed was wearing very old clothes, answered the door and politely greeted all of them. She then asked, "Is there something I can help you all with?"

The driver said, "We would like to talk to the owner of the house."

The lady said in response, "I am the owner of the house. My name is Elizabeth Griffin, and what are your names?"

The group said their names from left to right: Sarah Patterson, John Wilkinson, Lora Lopez, Steve Wilson, Marissa Miller, Benjamin Falconburg—"But most people call me Ben—Bruce Knightly, Leslie Newman, and Earl Montgomery, "At your service."

Then after the group introduced themselves to Elizabeth, she asked, "How exactly may I help you all?"

Earl replied with, "We were all hoping if you would let us stay at your house until the weather got a bit better. Is that okay with you?"

Elizabeth said in response, "Sure. Would all of you like to have a little tour of my house before I show everyone to the rooms you will be staying in for the rest of the day, as well as until the weather outside got better than it is right now?"

The group agreed to go on Elizabeth's tour of her house to see what she had in it and around it. While on the tour, everyone saw things that seemed obvious to have for a woman who was wearing clothes they all knew were worn by people around the 1700s and 1800s, and few other things surprised them too. The obvious items they saw was a living room that had a chimney made of bricks in the center, a long hallway that is mostly of wood, and several paintings on the walls of both the living and the hallway they were still going through that artists would consider to be cultural in a certain or specific way.

Also, the few items or things that surprised the group were that of more hallways as well as a second floor with the same number of hallways as the floor they were on, a very large kitchen, and a huge garden that was surrounded by glass with frames that seemed like some kind of black wood. Another thing the group saw about the garden is that it was connected to the kitchen.

A short while later, Elizabeth took everyone down a hallway and then said, "When we get to the rooms you will use for the night, all of you should know that everyone will have to decide on a assigning people into those rooms, but one of the rooms has only one bed while the others have four beds in each of them."

By the time the group got to the rooms Elizabeth was letting them use, Earl said, "Thanks for leading us to these rooms as well as letting us know that we have to set ourselves in the rooms especially the one with the single bed."

Elizabeth responded with, "You're welcome, and I will let all you go ahead in assigning each of you a room, even the single bedroom. So, everyone, have a good night."

Before she was too far away from the group, they told Elizabeth good night, and some thanked her for letting them stay in her house. Elizabeth turned around and answered with, "You're welcome."

When she was gone out of their sight, the group immediately started to set each other in the rooms.

The first room they had to assign someone in was the room with the single bed in it. Earl suddenly said, "I will take the large room with the single bed, if it is all right with everyone?"

Lora asked, "Why do you want to get that room?"

Earl replied, "Well, I have always been used to sleeping in a room by myself, and I don't want to change my sleeping customs for any reasons at all. Is that going to be a problem with anyone?"

The group shook their heads to answer Earl's question. After Earl was at his assigned room's door and was about to open the door, he turned his sights to the group and said, "Good luck with assigning each other to the rooms, and good night, everyone."

They said good night to Earl as well. By the time Earl closed his door behind him, the group had finally assigned every single one of them to each of the rooms.

In one room were John, Sarah, Ben, and Lora, while the other room had Bruce Leslie, Steve, and Marissa. Then before all of them went into their assigned rooms, they said good night to each other. After they shut their room's door behind them, everyone started to set themselves up to the beds in their rooms. In one room they set themselves up with the women on the front beds that were near their room's door while the men took the beds in the back.

In the other room, they set themselves up with the women on the beds to the left side of the room while the men on the beds to the right. A while later, when everyone was fast asleep, a loud scream suddenly went throughout the house. The group woke up and went outside their rooms. Some had a look of fright on their faces while the others were of shock and disbelief.

A moment later, Marissa asked, "Where is Earl?"

When the rest of the group saw Earl wasn't with them, they went to the door of his room. Ben knocked on Earl's door and said, "Earl, are you still asleep in bed?"

Chapter 2

Then after all of them didn't hear Earl answer, Ben unlocked the door and opened it. The group couldn't see anything in the room because it was in pitch-black darkness. Ben went inside the room first and told the others he was looking for a lamp or something to make everyone able to see if Earl is still in bed.

When Ben finally found a lamp, he clicked it on, and it gave light to most of the room. The light was good enough for all of them because they only needed to see if Earl was still asleep in bed. By the time, Ben had gotten to the bed and found out that Earl wasn't in bed. He went outside and told the group of what he found out.

Bruce replied, "If Earl isn't in his room or even his bed, then where could he possibly be?"

Lora then asked, "Do you think that the loud scream we heard could have been him?"

Everyone thought of what Lora said, and all thought it could be a possibility since Earl wasn't in his room as well as was nowhere to be seen. A moment later, John said, "Maybe we should split up and look for Earl wherever he might be."

Ben followed with, "That's a good idea, but how should we set up the search groups?"

Bruce answered, "Maybe we should go into groups of two with the people of both rooms. Does anyone else have another way of setting up the groups?"

The others thought it through and found that Bruce's way to set the groups was their only way to set them. When they finished setting their groups up, they found their concern now was where each of them was supposed to look for Earl.

Steve then said, "I think Sarah and John should look into the kitchen as well as the garden. Ben and Lora, look into the other hallways on this floor. Bruce and Leslie, look around the living room, while Marissa and I will go looking through the hallways on the second floor, if that's okay with everyone."

Everyone thought Steve's plan of action for each of the groups was brilliant and good in every way possible. A moment later, the groups went to their given places to find Earl and agreed to meet back in an hour in front of the rooms to see if any of them had luck in finding Earl.

A short while later, Sarah and John finally got to the kitchen, and immediately entered to look through both the kitchen and the garden.

After Sarah and John were in the kitchen, they both didn't see Earl in the kitchen, but one of them saw something else that caught their interest. John tapped Sarah on the shoulder and said, "Hey, look, there is something in the closet over there, and might be something interesting in there."

Sarah saw the glimmer John was telling her about, and asked, "What do you think it is?"

John replied, "Whatever it might be, it could be something useful for us."

They both went towards the closet to find out what the glimmer was.

When both of them got to the closet, Sarah saw what the glimmer was, and noticed something else in the closet. She told John, "Do you see that there are other things glimmering in the closet?"

After John noticed what Sarah was pointing out to him, he said, "We should go inside there and find a light switch of some kind so we can see what exactly these glimmering objects are."

A moment later, Sarah was hit by some kind of metallic cord at the center of the closet, and she checked what it really was. The moment she finally found out what it was, she gently pulled the cord down, and light suddenly went throughout the entire closet. By the time they were able to see what the glimmering items were, John said, "Wow, this is quite the collection of wine Elizabeth has, although I doubt it actually is hers."

Then Sarah asked, "What makes you think these bottles of wine are not Elizabeth's?"

John answered with, "Well, I haven't known that much women who collect as much wine to fill an entire closet with, so that's where I have my doubts that these are actually hers."

Sarah thought about it and figured that what John told her could be very true. After she found out that John had a right to have his doubts about the wine collection being Elizabeth's, Sarah said, ",Well if it isn't her, then who's the actual owner of these wine bottles?"

John said in response, "I would have to say that this belongs to Elizabeth's husband."

Sarah knew John had a point on the person who might be the actual owner of the wine bottles. When Sarah agreed with what John told her, they went out of the closet and began to go to the door that would take them to the garden. Then after they got to the door, both quickly entered into the garden. Sarah and John went separate ways to be able to cover and look thoroughly through the entire garden so they were completely sure whether Earl was or wasn't there as well.

A short while later, John found a shed that appeared to be old, and he saw most of it was covered with roots. He looked around the shed before he tried to get the doors open and see what it has inside. After John failed to open the doors, he suddenly saw an ax on the left side of the shed lying down on the ground as well as surrounded by roots. By the time John got the ax in his hands, he started to cut through all the roots that made it hard for him to open the shed doors.

Before he finished cutting all the roots out of the way of the shed doors, John heard a shriek and began to move toward it. Then he shouted, "Sarah, where are you?"

Out of nowhere, he heard, "John, help, something is dragging me somewhere possibly terrible, so please come and save me!"

John figured Sarah was somewhere in the center of the garden. He went there quickly to find out what was the thing that was dragging her away somewhere.

A moment later, John found drag marks on the ground. The marks looked like they came from a person's hands. He followed them to see if they came from Sarah. When John finally found her, he said, "Are you okay, Sarah?"

Sarah looked at him and replied, "Well, I'm currently fighting to not let this thing take me away somewhere, so if you don't mind, get this thing off my leg!"

John went to where one of her legs was being wrapped as well as pulled to some place that might be horrifying to think about.

After he was able to see what the thing dragging her was, John was both shocked and baffled by what it really was. John then said, "I found out what was pulling you away somewhere, but I don't think you will believe me if I told you."

Sarah followed with, "Are you serious? What can it be to make you say that?"

John said in response, "It's a root that is probably from one of these trees."

After he told her about what was the thing that was dragging him away, Sarah said, "This is not possible. Tree roots can't come alive and drag people away to someplace horrifying."

When John was set to cut the root off Sarah, he immediately started to chop the root with as much force he thought would be necessary to get free from the root's hold. A moment later, John finally got Sarah free from the root's grip and picked her up off the ground. Then after he got her back up on her feet, they both began to run toward the door to the kitchen.

A short while later, they were about to enter the kitchen when another root got hold of John's right leg and pulled him back into the garden right away. He fell to the ground hard and dropped the ax he was holding to the center of the kitchen. When the root started to pull him in with a bit of force, John grabbed on to the left side of the doorway with all his might.

THE HAUNTED HOUSE

Before Sarah could get the ax to help him out, like he did with her, John said, "Don't bother with the ax. We need to come up with something that will get rid of this problem for good."

Sarah then asked, "What do you think would be a good solution to this problem? Because I can't come up with one right now."

John answered with, "Get a wine bottle, a rag, and turn on the stove halfway."

After Sarah figured out what John's plan was, she went to the stove first to turn it on to the center of its dial. Then after she had the stove on halfway, Sarah quickly went to get a wine bottle and find a rag.

By the time Sarah finally had a wine bottle and found a rag nearby, she started to uncork the bottle and insert a corner of the rag into the passageway of the bottle. When she got the rag securely in the passageway of the bottle, Sarah ran to the stove to light the rag on fire. After Sarah had the rag on fire, she began to run to the doorway that went toward the garden as carefully as she could to avoid dropping the wine bottle, because she knew it would end badly if she were to do so.

A moment later, Sarah threw the wine bottle and saw it had hit what she thought was the center of the garden. The fire began to spread quickly throughout the garden. When the root finally released John from its hold, he and Sarah heard something that surprised and shocked them. Both of them heard what sounded like a shriek of pain and agony from out of nowhere. Sarah got John into the kitchen and then shut the door with the lock on.

After Sarah and John were inside the kitchen, they both watched the garden completely burning down to the ground. Suddenly, from out of nowhere, a root started to hit the center of the door's window. While the root was hitting the window, Sarah and John noticed something was trying to open the door, which told them another root was attempting to get into the kitchen and probably drag them into the burning garden.

The other root was not able to open the door since Sarah had locked the door, and knowing that, she was content in doing just that. A moment later, Sarah and John began to hear the shrieks they had heard before, but this time, the shrieks sounded a bit more worse. When the root that was hitting the door window finally made some serious damage to it, the root caught on fire and started to wiggle out of control.

Once the root caught on fire and was rapidly moving out of control, Sarah and John relaxed as they watched the entire garden burn down, and knew that they had gotten rid of their current problem for good. A short while later, Sarah and John were outside in the hallway when they felt a burning sensation coming from where the root had wrapped itself on the both of them.

They looked at their legs where both of them felt the burning sensation coming from and pulled up their pants on that leg, carefully to see what was making them feel this irritating sensation. When Sarah and John finally were able to see what the sensation was, they saw it looked like a rash in the form of a snake slithering up their legs.

After they saw what the burning sensation appeared to look like, Sarah said, "I will get a couple of rags and wet them so we could put them on those irritating rashes on our legs."

John nodded and said, "I think that's a great idea, and I can go with you so we could treat our marks at the same time when you get the rags wet."

Sarah agreed to let John go with her so they can treat both their annoying marks at the same time.

When Sarah finally got the rags wet, she gave one of them to John, and they both started to treat their irritating marks and tried to lessen the burning sensation on their legs to where they wouldn't be annoyed every time they walked. A moment later, Sarah and John began to walk back to the rooms they all slept in and see how the others did in their search for Earl.

Before they could go more down the hallway, Sarah and John heard a creak behind them. They felt a cool chill go down their backs.

By the time Sarah and John looked to see what the thing was that had made the creaking sound, they were both shocked and surprised to see two shadowy figures walking toward them progressively.

THE HAUNTED HOUSE

Once they saw the dark figures coming their way, John prepared to act fast if the shadowy figures tried to do any kind of harm to either of them when they were in range to do such things to them.

Chapter 3

When the shadowy figures were close and one of them reached out for Sarah, John was about to hit it with the ax when the dark figure told him to not hit him. He recognized the person's voice right away. "Bruce, is that really you?"

Bruce answered with, "Yes, it's me, as well as Leslie."

Then Sarah said, "Are you two coming from the living room?"

Leslie replied with, "Yes, we are, and neither of us was able to find Earl there."

John followed with, "Well, if you two are heading back the rooms right now, we should go there together since we are heading there as well."

Leslie and Bruce agreed to walk to the rooms with Sarah and John, and began to do so immediately. A while later, all of them finally got to the rooms and noticed they were the only ones at the rooms. After they saw that, Sarah said, "I think we should go into one of the rooms and wait for the others to come by the rooms."

The others thought about it for a short moment and agreed to Sarah's idea to wait for everyone else in one of the rooms. By the time they were in the room to their right and were waiting for the others for quite some time, all of them started to hear footsteps and a faint chatter going through the hallway. Then after all of them heard those things, they went outside to find out what was making those footsteps and chatter.

THE HAUNTED HOUSE

After they were in the hallway as well as outside the room, all of them looked in the direction where the footsteps and chatter were coming from. When all of them saw two dark figures, Sarah shouted, "Who's there? Who are you two?"

A moment later, one of them responded with, "It's us, Marissa and I."

Then following the moment the others heard that the two dark figures really were Marissa and Steve, they waited for them to get to where all of them were standing.

When Marissa and Steve finally got to where the others were standing at, they started to tell them how their search for Earl went. Marissa and Steve told everyone their search for Earl in the second floor hallways was of no use, for they were not able to find him. Bruce asked everyone to go into the room they were in before and wait again for the rest of them as well as to see if they had any luck in finding Earl than they all had in doing so.

The moment everyone was in the room, John asked Steve and Marissa if they saw or found anything interesting in the hallways on the second floor.

Marissa said in response, "Well, we found several boxes filled with a lot of matchboxes in some of the rooms in two of the hallways on the second floor."

Steve added, "We also saw a strange door that gave us a strange feeling every we took when we walked towards that door."

Bruce then asked, "What occurred by the time the both of you got to the door?"

Marissa answered with, "We both tried opening the door, but it seemed to be locked up pretty tight."

After Marissa said that to them, Sarah asked, "What do you think could be behind that door that was giving both of you a strange as well as weird feeling?"

Steve replied with, "Probably something bad, or possibly even evil, to be giving us a weird feeling when we were getting near the door."

Bruce then said, "What did the weird sensation feel like for the both of you?"

They looked at each other as well as nod, and then Marissa said, "It felt dark and shallow. It was as if we were feeling the sensation of suffering and sorrow of several people in one place."

Steve continued with, "Which gave us chills that went down our backs."

When they told the others that, some of them felt a bit frightened while the rest felt intrigued and quite interested in that door on the second floor.

A short while later, everyone began to hear footsteps go through the hallway once more, and to them, it meant Lora and Ben were at last coming back to the rooms, as they had all agreed to do so the moment they finished searching their assigned as well as given area for Earl. When all of them were outside in the hallway again, they tried to see if it really were Lora and Ben coming back to the rooms or something else that might be bad for everyone.

A moment later, everyone was able to see what was coming toward them, and they saw that they were actually Lora and Ben. A few of them were happy to see Lora and Ben were finally coming back to where they were, while the rest also noticed both of them were dragging something covered and were leaving behind a dark trail while they were moving toward everyone.

Another thing some of them noticed was that Lora had an expression on her face that seemed blank and gloomy. After Lora and Ben finally got to where everyone was standing, Steve asked, "What happened during your search for Earl in the hallways on this floor, and what exactly are you two dragging in those covers to be making a dark trail while both of you were coming towards us?"

Lora and Ben looked at each other with a grim look on their faces, and Ben said in response, "We found Earl in the middle hallway at the end of it."

After Ben said that to everyone, Leslie said, "Well, that's great news. Where is Earl then?"

Lora answered, "Well, you won't believe us when we tell you all where he is right now."

Leslie responded with, "Where could Earl possibly be that we wouldn't believe either of you when you tell us?"

Ben then said, "Well then, Earl is inside the covers, and he is also dead."

When everyone heard what Ben told them about where Earl was, all of them thought that they were being played with some kind of joke about Earl's whereabouts. Then John said, You both can't be serious, because if Earl is really dead inside those covers, then what is that trail the thing you have in there has been leaving behind every move the both of you have made to get back to the rooms, like we all agreed to do after finishing our search area thoroughly?"

Lora looked down with her eyes closed, and Ben followed with, "It's blood. Earl's blood, because he was missing something vital from his body when we found him."

Sarah then asked, "What was vitally missing from Earl's body?"

Ben answered with, "Earl was missing his head, and we weren't able to ever find his head anywhere in that hallway."

Steve chuckled and said in response, "If what you are telling us is true, then show us what's inside the covers, if you don't mind."

Lora and Ben looked at each other for a short moment and slowly began to open the covers to show everyone what was inside. When everyone was able to see what was inside the covers and saw it really was Earl without his head, most were horrified while the rest were shocked by what all of them were seeing.

After everyone saw Earl's headless body in the covers, the women went to the guys' chests to cover their eyes completely while the men attempted to comfort them through something that might have been both horrifying and a mentally scarring moment for them. A moment later, Lora and Ben closed the covers and laid it down on the floor.

When they finally had the covers completely on the floor, John said, We should go into the room and try to get ourselves together, okay?"

Everyone nodded, agreeing with John's idea, while Ben asked all of them which room they were going to go in. After everyone pointed to the room to their right, they began to progressively enter the room in an orderly fashion.

By the time everyone was inside the room, the men allowed the women to have some time by themselves or with the other women in whatever part of the room, and the men stood somewhere nearby to help them in any way they could. A while later, the group started to hear a wailing sound go through the hallway. Some of them also heard a cry for help at the same time as the wailing sound went on.

Everyone went outside into the hallway again and tried to see who or what was making those cries for help. When they got in the hallway, all of them didn't see anything, but the cries continued to go through the hallway. A moment later, a bright light suddenly came out from the entryway of the hallway. It made everyone cover their eyes with their arms. Then by the time the light lessened, the group was finally able to see and find out whatever was making the bright light.

The moment everyone was able to see what the bright light was, they were all shocked. The group was without words by what the bright light appeared to be to all of them.

Ben said, "Earl, is it really you?"

After Ben said that to what appeared to be the appariton of Earl, the apparition looked at the group with a very grim expression on its face. The apparition looked at Ben and smiled, as if it was happy to see him.

Then the apparition replied with, "Yes, it's me, everyone, and as you all can see, I'm a living ghost."

After Earl's ghost said that to the group, Bruce followed with, "What happened to you that would end up making you into an apparition?"

Earl's ghost answered with, "Well, I wasn't able to sleep, so I went for a little walk, but when I did, I saw Elizabeth and talked to her for a moment."

Earl's ghost continued to tell the group what had occurred before he became an apparition of himself. He got to a part that seemed quite strange to most of the people in the group. It was when Earl was following Elizabeth to a restroom, and when he lost focus of her, she disappears from out of nowhere. Earl then saw a shadow quickly enter a room up ahead of him. He ran to the room the shadow went

THE HAUNTED HOUSE

inside of. When Earl got a few feet away from the room, he continued on to the room.

By the time Earl finally got to the room, he saw the room was pitch-black. Suddenly, from inside the room, Earl began to hear a growl that sounded like a vicious animal. Then Earl said that when he entered the room, some creature pounced at him and everything went dark after it attacked him.

After Earl finished telling the group what had happened to him, John said, "Then there has to be something supernatural about this house because everyone here knows that apparitions don't exist, especially ones people can see with their own eyes."

Everyone thought about what John told them and agreed his conclusion was the only one that explained why Earl's apparition was appearing before all of them. Then after everyone accepted what was happening around them, Earl started to scream sounds of pain and agony, which startled as well as frightened some of the people in the group.

After Earl's screams of pain and agony continued, Bruce asked, "What is happening, Earl? Why are you screaming in pain?"

Earl's ghost responded with, "I don't know what exactly is happening to me, but it feels as if someone is brutally torturing me somehow." When he stopped screaming, he immediately began to disappear into thin air.

Chapter 4

The moment Earl disappeared completely, the group tried to figure out who or what can be able to torture an apparition so badly. Then all of a sudden, the group finally noticed both the covers that had Earl's body in it, as well as the trail of blood, were somehow gone. After everyone noticed that, they all thought about what to do next since all of them now knew what happened to Earl and that something or someone is somewhere in this house with supernatural capabilities, and is probably going to come after all of them since it had already taken one of them both body and soul.

Then Ben said, "Does anyone have any ideas as to what can be capable of killing someone in the blink of an eye as well as being able to torture a spirit?"

John said in response, "I think I do, but it's not a *what*, it's a *who*."

Lora asked, "What do you mean by that?"

John replied with, "I'm saying that I might know who is behind Earl's death, but you all will probably won't believe me if I did tell you."

Lora followed with, "Just tell us so we can know who you think is behind Earl's death, and we will see how we all react to what you are going to tell us."

John then answered with, "I think the one behind Earl's death is Elizabeth."

When everyone heard what John told them, they were all shocked. A moment later, Steve asked, "What makes you think that Elizabeth is behind Earl's death?"

John said in response, "The reason why I think that Elizabeth is behind Earl's death is because she was the only one that was with him, and he was following her to a restroom until he last saw her."

The moment the group heard what John told them, they remembered what Earl's apparition told them what had occurred after he lost sight of Elizabeth. They tried to think about it.

They thought about it thoroughly so as not to miss anything that might concur with John's conclusion. After the group finally finished thinking thoroughly about Earl's last moments before he was killed and became an apparition himself, they found out John was right about making Elizabeth the main culprit of Earl's death.

Then after the group had their thoughts altogether about Earl's incident and the person behind it, Ben said, "What should we do now? Because I think we have to come up with some kind of plan of action, for Elizabeth might possibly come after us next, doesn't everyone agree?"

When the others heard what Ben said to them, all of them thought of ways to avoid getting attacked by whatever Elizabeth really was.

By the time one of them came up with a plan, Bruce said, "I think I have a plan of action, but it might seem extreme to most of you."

Sarah then asked, "Tell us what your plan of action is, and we will see if it's extreme or not."

Bruce answered with, "My plan of action involves us burning this house down to the ground with whatever we can use to do so."

The others were shocked by Bruce's plan of action to avoid getting killed by whatever Elizabeth's true form was. When everyone was calm and collected, Leslie asked, "What made you come up with such a plan of action that sounds quite extreme?"

Bruce said in response, "Well, I thought that there might be something evil possessing this entire house, so burning it down to the ground is what I came up with."

The group thought if they should really go through with burning this evil house. A couple of them remembered something that occurred to them while they were looking for Earl, and everyone, which includes them, also put what all of them experienced when Earl's apparition appeared before them. A moment later, the group agreed to go through Bruce's plan of action. They would help him all the way until the evil house was nothing but ash.

Then Bruce said, "Well, the first thing we need is something that would help all of us with burning down the house. Does anyone have a suggestion on the subject?"

John said, "Sarah and I found a closet filled with wine bottles. We could use them to burn the house."

After everyone heard what John told them, they agreed to use the wine bottles to burn the entire house, and started to walk to the kitchen right away.

A short while later, the group finally got to the kitchen and immediately went inside to get the wine bottles from the closet. When every single one of them had a couple of wine bottles in their hands, Ben asked, "What else should we get? Because we can't burn the whole house with wine by itself."

John answered with, "I know that. We could cut some rags up and put them in the bottles' passageway."

Sarah followed with, "Then we could turn on the stove and use it to light up the rags."

The group thought about what John and Sarah had told them for a moment to see if it was a great idea. When everyone went to get a rag for each of them, they each cut the rags into six pieces and put two of those in the bottles' passageway.

Before Sarah could turn on the stove, Ben said, "Wait, Sarah, I don't think it's a good idea to light the rags with the stove anymore."

Sarah asked, "Why do you think that, Ben?"

Ben said in response, "Because if we did light the rags, we couldn't go that far before the bottle explodes."

After the group heard that, they all realized Ben made a very good point about what might occur to the bottles if they did light the rags.

THE HAUNTED HOUSE

Then John said, "If we can't use the stove to light the rags, then what else can we use to do that?"

Steve replied with, "What about the matchboxes Marissa and I found in the two hallways on the second floor?"

The group thought about it for a moment and found it a good idea to light the rags and burn whatever part of the house they each chose to do so.

A while later, the group was finally on the second floor, and was also trying to find a way to speed up the search for the matchboxes in the two hallways.

Then John said, "We should form into two groups of four to search the rooms in the two hallways Marissa and Steve found them in."

The group agreed to do that and set themselves in the order of the group's arrival to the room from first to last.

After they got themselves in the groups, all of them immediately went into the two hallways Steve and Marissa had pointed out to the others. When Sarah's group got to the first two rooms, she and John went into these rooms to search for the matchboxes while the rest searched for them in the other two rooms. In the meantime, Marissa's group was doing the same but was a bit faster as well as more thorough.

By the time they had found matchboxes in their rooms, all of them put as many matchboxes as they could in their pockets. A moment later, when Sarah's group was in the middle of their hallway with pockets filled with matchboxes, they all began to feel something that seemed very uncomfortable to all of them. After they felt this strange sensation, they remembered what Marissa and Steve had told them about the door that was giving them an unsettling feeling while they were in the hall and had gotten close to the room.

When they realized where all of them were in, Sarah shouted, "Marissa, I think you and the others should come where we are all at, because we are experiencing something very strange!"

The moment Marissa's group got to where Sarah and the others were, they all immediately started to feel a very gloomy sensation. After Marissa's group felt that sensation, she said, "We are all in the hallway with the locked door that gives out a dark and gloomy sensation throughout the hall."

Then Steve asked, "Do all of you want to check out the door yourselves to find out if we were telling everyone the truth?"

Once everyone agreed to check out the door to see if the sensation they were all feeling does get stronger every time they got closer to the door, all of them began to feel the dark sensation get more intense with every step they took toward the door.

By the time everyone got to the door at last, Ben went to the door and tried to open it as well as. When Ben attempted to open the door, he discovered the door was locked and felt the unsettling sensation got even stronger than before. When everyone felt that the sensation had gotten even more powerful, Steve said, "Ben, I think since you are not able to open either, we should go back to the kitchen and figure out what parts of the house should burn next since someone has already burned down the garden."

John said in response, "You noticed that, Steve? Well, that was the doing of Sarah and I, but mostly Sarah."

Sarah followed with, "There was something attacking us, and we later found out that the thing that was attacking us was something that everyone here knows can't attack people at all."

Then Marissa asked, "What was the thing attacking you both turned out to be in the end?"

Sarah replied with, "It was a tree's root, and we were both shocked and in disbelief when we found that out."

After everyone heard what Sarah told them about what had attacked both her and John while they were in the garden, John said, "It was after we were both attacked by the tree root that we decided to make sure that it would not attack anyone else, so we burned it down to make sure it wouldn't be able to do so."

After Sarah and John cleared the others of the reason why they had burned the garden, everyone thought about what they might face ahead and of more reason to burn every part of the house. When the group got their thoughts together about going through with burning the house down, Steve said, "Well, let us hurry up and get those wine bottles and start burning this accursed house."

A moment later, the group finally got back to the kitchen and got the bottles they already had set up, as well as more wine bottles. After everyone finished setting up more wine bottles, Marissa said, "Let us get some bags to carry all these wine bottles, because it would be quite difficult to carry these bottles in our arms, don't you agree?"

When the group agreed to do Marissa's idea, they quickly looked for bags to carry all the wine bottles they were going to have with them. The moment one of them found some bags, Sarah said, "Hey, everyone, I found several bags and they also seem to be made of some kind of leathery fabric."

When Ben got to where Marissa was at, he took a closer look at what she was telling everyone about and find out what the bags really were.

After Ben found out what the bags were exactly, he said, "The bags are made of leather and are also the kind of bags people take to a food market of any kind."

Then after everyone heard what Ben told them about the bags as well as what they were made of, all of them wanted one of those bags to put all their wine bottles in. Ben quickly gave the others a bag to carry their bottles and put them carefully in the bags they will have.

When everyone had their bags and their bottles in them as well, the group had to now to decide what part of the house their groups should go to burn. By the time the group finally knew where they should go to burn, all of them went into the groups they were in when they were all looking for Earl.

A short while later, Ben and Lora were back in the hallway where they found Earl's body and started to go through each of the rooms in the hall. While they were looking through the rooms in the hall, Lora saw something on the far end of the room she had stopped at. After she saw that unknown thing, she said, "Hey, Ben, I found something interesting in this room, but I can't see what it is." When Ben was at the room Lora was standing outside of, he said, "Well, let's go inside and find out what it is you found interesting in this room."

The moment Lora agreed to go inside the room with Ben, they went into the room and noticed something about the wall Lora talked about. There were what appeared to them portrait frames, but they couldn't see what they had in the center of them. After they saw that, Ben and Lora began to look for something to light up the room so they can be able to see what were in the center of each of the portrait frames. A moment later, Ben found what felt to him like some kind of lamp, and immediately turned the knob on the lamp.

Chapter 5

When the lamp lit the entire room, Ben and Lora looked at all the portrait frames to find out what they all had in the center of them. The moment Ben and Lora saw what all the portraits had in the center of them, they were both shocked and surprised by what they were. The portraits had pictures of Elizabeth with different men, and one of them had a kid in the picture.

Lora then asked, "What could these pictures be to have Elizabeth in all of them with different men and one with a kid?"

Ben noticed something at the bottom of the portrait frames, and said, "Look, Lora, there is something attached to the bottom of each of the frames."

After Lora also saw what Ben noticed on the bottom of the portrait frames, they both went toward the portraits to see what was on the bottom of the frames.

When they finally got to the portrait frames, Ben and Lora each looked at each of the frames to find out what exactly was attached on the bottom of the frames. Once Ben and Lora finally saw what was attached to the portrait frames, they found out each had a small plaque on them as well as something intriguing written on them.

Each plaque had Elizabeth's name, the men's name, the kids' name, and probably the date each of the portraits was taken. Another thing they noticed about the plaques was mostly the dates on each of them had a ten- to twenty-year difference between them. After Ben and Lora saw that on the plaques, they also found out the picture frame with the kid was the last portrait taken.

Then Lora opened one of her wine bottles and started to place small drops of the wine on parts of the room that would catch on fire quickly as well as spread the fire throughout the whole room. A moment later, before Lora was going to light the wine trail she had made with a single wine bottle, Ben quickly took down the portraits and took them outside the room to show the others what they found in one of their rooms.

Once Ben finally had the portraits outside the room, Lora lit a match and dropped it on the wine trail. Then after the trail caught on fire, the fire rapidly spread throughout the entire room, and they stood outside the room, watching it burn. After the whole room was on fire, Ben and Lora continued to go through the rest of the rooms and left the portraits in the middle of the hallway while they were doing so.

A short while later, Ben and Lora had lit on fire half of the rooms with most of their wine bottles. They quickly finished burning the remaining rooms of the hallway, and did so carefully as well as with precision to throw the lit wine bottles at a place in each of the rooms, where the fire could spread real fast with the help of the wine.

By the time Ben and Lora had finally finished burning all the rooms in the entire hall, they went to pick up the portraits and go back to the kitchen to get more wine bottles. When they got to the kitchen, Lora went to get a couple of rags, and Ben took both bags to fill them up with more wine bottles. The moment Ben had both bags completely filled with wine bottles, Lora found two rags and then got a knife to cut them into several pieces.

After Ben got to where Lora was at, he opened the passageway of all the wine bottles so she could put all the rag pieces into them and go see what parts of the house the others hadn't burned down. After they had all the wine bottles set up, Ben and Lora had an unexpected encounter with two familiar people.

Lora then said, "Hey, Bruce and Leslie, how did burning the living room go for the both of you?"

Leslie answered with, "Well, it went very well and went without a hitch or any kind of disturbance,"

Bruce followed with, "There were also shelves that didn't spread from top to bottom, but it was quite easy to resolve that issue. How did you two do in burning your part of the house?"

Ben said in response, "It went great. We used all the wine bottles we had and found something interesting in one of the rooms."

Bruce then asked, "What did the two of you discover in a room that you find interesting?"

Lora replied with, "We found a few portraits of Elizabeth with different men and one with a little boy."

After Lora said that to Bruce and Leslie, they both had a surprised look on their faces. Ben and Lora noticed, and Ben asked, "What's wrong? Why do the both of you have those surprised looks on your faces?"

Leslie said in response, "We found a portrait of Elizabeth and a man, but we didn't see it before because it was hidden with a leather cloth."

After she said that, Lora then asked, "Did it have a plaque at the bottom of the frame?"

Leslie responded with, "Yes, it did, How did you know that?"

Ben answered with, "Because we also found them on the portraits we found in the room."

Lora followed with, "Did the plaque have Elizabeth's name, the man's name, and the date of the portrait?"

Bruce and Leslie both nodded in answer to the question. After they answered Lora's question, Ben then said, "What did the plaque say exactly?"

Leslie answered with, "James and Elizabeth Griffin. March 5, 1816."

When Ben and Lora heard what Leslie told them, they were both shocked and surprised by it. Then Lora said, "That would make that portrait the oldest compared to the ones we found."

Bruce replied with, "Are you serious? You are telling us that the portrait we found is the first and oldest one than the ones you two found in the room altogether?"

Ben said in response, "Yes, we are, because the other portraits had different dates, and they each had a specific timeline difference as well."

Lora followed with, "And with the date you saw on the portrait, there is a bit more time difference compared to the others." After Lora said that to Bruce and Leslie, they both wondered what could have been the oldest portrait Lora and Ben found in the room.

The moment Leslie asked them what the oldest portrait they found in the room, Ben then said, "The date on that was July 17 of 1841."

After Bruce and Leslie heard that, they figured the time difference between the two portraits was twenty-five years and wanted to know the dates of the other portraits Ben and Lora found.

Then Leslie asked, "What were the dates on the other portraits you two found?"

Lora answered with, "August 8 of 1856, June 11 of 1871, September 21 of 1886, April 15 of 1901, and December 4 of 1916."

After Leslie finished telling the dates of the other portraits to Ben and Lora, they noticed the time difference between all the portraits altogether.

When Bruce and Leslie had that figured out about the portraits, Ben asked, "Did you take the portrait with you before burning the living room?"

Bruce said in response, "I'm sorry to say this, but we couldn't take the portrait with us because we weren't able to take it down from where it was."

Lora then said, "Why do you say that? Why were you not able to take the portrait down?"

Leslie replied with, "We weren't able to take it down no matter what we did or used."

Bruce followed with, "It was like the portrait was glued or cemented to the wall it was on, so we left it to burn along with the living room."

After Bruce said that, Ben asked, "Do the two of you want to come with us in burning another part of the house?"

Lora continued with, "And if you want to, both of you can restock on wine bottles, and we can wait for you two while you do that."

Bruce and Leslie thought about it for a moment and then agreed to go with Ben and Lora. A moment later, Bruce and Leslie were quickly restocking their wine bottles' count, which wasn't much, before going with Ben and Lora to another part of the house to burn down. When they finished restocking wine bottles, both of them went to where Ben and Lora were standing at and immediately went to wherever they wanted to go to next to burn.

By the time Ben and the others were at the center of the entire house where the stairs to the second floor were as well, they went toward the hallway that was in front of the stairs but saw something that was going through the hallway. Smoke was going through the entire hallway. This sight puzzled all of them as to why there was smoke there.

Ben asked, "Did you all notice the smoke going through that hallway before? Because I didn't."

Bruce said in response, "No, we didn't notice the hallway that is filled with smoke."

Leslie followed with, "But before there was smoke going through the hallway, Bruce and I did see Sarah and John go into it."

Ben and Lora thought since Sarah and John were the only ones seen going into that hallway, they must have been the ones who created the smoke by burning the rooms.

Another thing they noticed about the smoke was it appeared to be coming from the first few rooms in the hallway. After they noticed those things, Lora said, "I think Sarah and John are still in that hallway."

Bruce replied with, "What makes you think that they are still in the hallway with all that smoke?"

Ben answered with, "Did anyone see that the smoke is coming from the nearest rooms from where we are all at right now?"

Then after Ben told the others of what he had seen about the smoke in the hallway, Bruce and Leslie tried to see if what he noticed about the smoke was absolutely true. When they finished figuring out about the smoke in the hallway, all of them found what Ben told them was true. The moment they discovered what Ben had pointed out to them was very accurate, Leslie said, "You're absolutely right, Ben. The smoke is coming from the closest rooms towards us."

Bruce followed with, "But if they really are still in that hallway, where do you think the two of them could in there with all that smoke?"

Ben answered with, "Well, since the smoke is coming from the rooms closest to us, they might be somewhere deeper inside the hallway."

The others thoroughly thought about what Ben said for a moment. When they finished thinking about it, all of them found out that Ben's explanation as to where Sarah and John might still be in the smoke-filled hallway was a very good point.

Chapter 6

A moment later, Leslie asked, "Should we go in that hallway and find out if they really are still in there, even with all the smoke?"

Ben responded with, "Well, if we want to know if they are somewhere farther inside the hallway, we need to go inside the hall to do so."

The others thought Ben was right, and told him to go right ahead with going into the hallway and see if Sarah and John are still in there.

By the time all of them entered the hallway, they saw the two rooms on both sides were the only ones on fire while the others weren't. After they saw that, each of them quickly went to the other rooms and checked them to see if either Sarah or John was in them. When everyone got to the last four rooms in the hallway, they all went into those rooms as fast as they could.

After they finished checking the last few rooms in the hall, everyone started to notice the smoke was coming toward them and that it seemed the smoke was a bit thicker than before. Once everyone saw the smoke had gotten thicker than it was before, they were about to go through the smoke so all of them could get back to the center of the house before they saw something strange happening to the smoke.

The smoke seemed to be moving in the motion of a snake moving around to make some kind of ball. Then out of the ordinary, the smoke appeared to have made a human face, an act that baffled most, while the rest were shocked by that appearance in the smoke. After they saw the face the smoke somehow created, it began to open its eyes and looked at everyone as if to study all of them.

Suddenly, the face smiled, and the others felt as if it was a smile of excitement over doing something evil and horrible to them. When they felt the sensation of evil intentions to them after seeing the smoke that now had human face make a quite demented smile, it began to get closer to them. When it was halfway to getting to where everyone was at, the smoke suddenly added very sharp teeth to its mouth that can be compared to the teeth of every savage animal there are in the world.

After everyone saw that happen from out of nowhere, Leslie asked, "What should we do? Because if we don't come up with a plan fast, I think that strange and creepy cloud of smoke will probably kill us."

A moment later, Ben said, "We can use the wine bottles to make way for us to get out of this hallway."

The others thought Ben's idea could work for all of them to escape out of the hallway they were in.

Everyone agreed to do Ben's plan of action to make way for them with the wine bottles they all had. Before they started to use the wine bottles to make a path to the center of the house as well as out of the hallway, Leslie then asked, "How exactly should we throw the bottles? Because I think we should also burn this hallway down too."

The group thought about it thoroughly to have an idea that they could agree on.

Once Bruce came up with something, he said, "Ben and Lora can throw the bottles to the side floors in front of us while Leslie and I do the same, but to the walls instead."

The others realized Bruce had come up with an excellent idea, and all agreed to go through with it so they can escape from being eaten by the demonic cloud of smoke in front of them.

By the time, all of them began to light the rag on the wine bottles they were about to throw toward the smoke in specific places and followed with throwing them to those given places. When everyone was halfway through the hallway, which was burning up as well, each of them thought they were all going escape without any kind of problem or complication.

Soon after they were almost out of the hallway, the cloud of smoke suddenly tried to attack them with a monstrous hand. All of them dropped to the floor to avoid the attack except Ben, who wasn't fast enough to avoid it. After Ben got hit by the cloud of smoke's attack by its monstrous hand it had made quickly, he was slammed against the wall hard, and he grunted in pain.

When he started to fall off the wall, Ben landed on top of shards of glass as well as the burning wine with his left arm and some parts of his body on that side of his body too. Ben immediately started to scream loudly in both pain and extreme agony, a sound that disturbed most of the others. Bruce quickly went to help Ben with the pain in any way he could figure out to do so. When Lora and Leslie tried to also help out Ben with the pain, Bruce stopped them and told the two to continue with clearing the way out of this hallway.

Then after Lora and Leslie agreed to continue making the way to escape the hallway and do so right away, Bruce was progressively succeeding in lessening Ben's pain as well as calming him down in the process. The moment Ben was finally calm as he could possibly be in his current condition, Bruce saw the others were almost finished with making the path out of the hallway.

The moment he saw that, Bruce carried Ben in his arms and started to walk down the path Lora and Leslie had continued to make. After the others threw the last bottles to at last escape the hallway they were all in right now, the cloud of smoke made a monstrous as well as a beastly wail that freaked out some of the group.

A moment later, everyone was finally out of the hallway, and right away, they looked for a place to set Ben down to then try to treat all his injuries and burns as much as they could. When the group got Ben on the kitchen table as well as taken off his shirt to see how serious the injuries were, everyone went to look for things that would help treat them very well.

After all of them found items and tools that would help them treat Ben's injuries and burns, Bruce began to use the pliers he had to take out all the shards of glass that Ben fell on, and Lora followed with pouring some alcohol on the open wounds caused by the glass shards.

When Lora finished putting the alcohol onto the open wounds, Leslie put small stacked pieces of rags in the wounds and wrapped them all up with table covers she tore apart into sleeves.

By the time Leslie was completely done with wrapping the sleeves of table covers very well on the stacked rag pieces covering the wounds, Ben appeared to have calmed down a bit and also seemed to be more relaxed than he was before. Then Bruce asked, "How are you feeling right now, Ben?"

Ben answered with, "I feel a bit more better than I was before, but I'm still feeling pain emanating from most of the left side of my body that was affected by the fall onto the fire, as well as glass shards, so thanks for treating them as best as you all were able to with the items and tools you found around the kitchen."

Everyone told Ben welcome for giving thanks for them helping and treating all his injuries and burns. Lora then helped Ben up off the table progressively as to not make any of his injuries or wounds any more worse than they already were. After Ben was on his feet and felt all right enough to walk, he then asked, "What should we do now?"

Bruce responded with, "We are going to take you to the shuttle bus where you will stay until we find the others and finish burning this demonic house."

Ben thought and right away realized he wouldn't be able to help anyone in his current condition. Then after Ben agreed to do Bruce's plan for him to go to the shuttle bus and wait until everyone has burned every part of the evil house, Lora said, "Do you think it's a good idea to take Ben out to the shuttle bus with how the weather is outside?"

Bruce told them if they haven't noticed yet that it has stopped raining outside and it also had gotten a little bit better. After the others found Bruce was telling the truth about how it has stopped raining and also seemed a bit better outside than it was when it was

THE HAUNTED HOUSE

raining, they were about to go on the way to the front door before all of them were confronted with two familiar faces once again.

Leslie said, "Hey, Marissa, how did you and Steve do with burning the hallways on the second floor?"

Marissa replied with, "We burned down all the hallways except one, and it was difficult to burn or go anywhere near or inside it."

Everyone figured out what hallway Marissa was telling them about. Lora then asked, "Did either of you feel something strange or experience something weird when the two of you got near it?"

Steve answered with, "Yes, we did. It felt like something or someone was going to come out of somewhere in that hallway and try to kill us both."

Marissa followed with, "And when we began to throw the bottles in the hallway, while standing at the entryway, both of us saw that it never caught on fire with any of the bottles we had and threw in it."

Bruce said in response, "What did the two of you do by the time you ran out of wine bottles?"

Steve replied with, "We started to walk back here to see if anyone else finished burning down their given part of this place, and that is when we caught up to all of you."

The moment Marissa noticed Ben's appearance, she asked, "What in the world happened to Ben?"

Lora answered, "You wouldn't believe is even if we told the both of you."

Steve then said, "What could it be now that all of you think we wouldn't believe any of you even after seeing Earls apparition?"

Bruce responded, "We were all going down a hallway we thought Sarah and John were in since Ben and Lora saw them go in it, but none of us saw them come out, just smoke."

Leslie continued with, "When we searched for them in every part of that hallway but didn't find them, we were all then attacked by a cloud of smoke that took the appearance of a person's face."

Marissa replied with, "What did you all do to avoid that strange cloud of smoke?"

Lora answered with, "We all threw the wine bottles each of us had at the cloud of smoke to both avoid its attack towards us and to get out of that hallway, but it then tried to hit us with a monstrous hand it made."

Ben then said, "I was the only one that the monster hand hit, and then I got even more injured when I fell on the ground."

Marissa then asked, "What happened when you fell to the ground that you got even more hurt than the hit by the monster hand the cloud of smoke created to attack all of you?"

Ben answered with, "I fell on top of burning wine and glass shards of the bottles we had already thrown."

Lora followed with, "We quickly took him to the kitchen so we could try to treat all of his injuries and burns as best as we could with the items and tools we found in the kitchen."

Then Steve asked, "Did the treatment help him out with his injuries and burns?"

Bruce responded with, "Well, as far as we can see, it appears to have lessened the pain Ben was feeling from his injuries and burns, but it didn't stop the pain completely, so we are taking him to the shuttle bus where he will wait until every single one of us have burned this entire house down to the ground."

A moment later, Marissa said, "Would any of you mind if we go to the shuttle bus with all of you?"

Leslie replied with, "No, we don't mind if you two come along with us."

Before all of them went to the front door, Leslie picked up the ax Sarah left in the kitchen when they each went to their given places to burn with the wine bottles.

When everyone got to the front door, Bruce opened the door for the others, and all of them saw how outside the house turned out to by the rainy weather. The grounds surrounding the entire house as far as they were all able to see was damp except the path that led to the main gate. Ben and Lora led everyone to the main gate on the path that wasn't damp as the grounds.

When they were halfway to the main gate, a few of them began to notice something moving in the grounds. Another thing they noticed was it was moving in the direction of Ben and Lora. Steve then said, "Hey, guys, there is something moving in the grounds that is heading towards those in the front."

Chapter 7

By the time Ben and Lora checked to see what Steve was telling them about, a couple of thick roots came out of the ground and got a hold on both of their legs. After the roots had a hold on Ben's and Lora's legs, it pulled them into the damp grounds in the direction of a line of trees that were far to the side of where they were standing at.

The others ran toward Ben and Lora to rescue them and try to free them from the roots' hold on their legs before it tried to do same the root in the garden attempted to do to both John and Sarah. When Steve and Marissa got a hold of Ben's and Lora's hand, they immediately started to pull them back toward them.

While they were doing that, Leslie went to where the roots had a grip on Ben and Lora. The moment Leslie got there, she decided on which root to cut first and seemed to be having a difficult time doing so. Then Bruce said, "Cut the root that is holding Ben first, and then do the same thing to the one on Lora."

Leslie asked about what Bruce told her and right away realized why she said that. After Leslie agreed to cut the root on Ben's leg first, she quickly started to cut it with all her force so to then immediately cut the one on Lora's leg as well. A moment later, Leslie finished cutting the root on Ben's leg, and right away began to cut the root on Lora's leg with as much force she could still use to do so.

The moment Ben was freed from the roots' hold, Marissa got closer to him and asked, "Ben, how are you feeling?."

THE HAUNTED HOUSE

Ben answered with, "I'm feeling a bit more in pain than I was before."

Marissa realized why that was and tried to carefully inspect his wounds to see if any of them have gotten worse than it was before they were treated.

After seeing that a few of Ben's wounds have worsened, Marissa said, "Hey, everyone, some of Ben's wounds have gotten worse."

By the time the others heard what Marissa told them, Lora was finally free from the roots' hold at last. Bruce went to where Marissa was at and checked Ben's wounds himself to see how much they have worsened.

After Bruce finished checking the condition of Ben's wounds, he told some of the group to go ahead and set things up at the shuttle bus while the rest help him take Ben there. A while later, Bruce and the others who helped him take Ben to the shuttle bus were finally there, and the rest who went ahead to set things up in the shuttle had done so very well.

Bruce asked everyone if one of them could go into the shuttle to make sure Ben doesn't make any of his wounds get even worse than they already are by going into the shuttle by himself. Lora quickly volunteered to do so and went into the shuttle to position herself for when Ben was going to enter it. Before she got into the shuttle, Lora stretched out her hand to him for her to help him get in without straining himself too much, and he accepted the help.

The moment Ben was at last in the shuttle, he sat down and tried to relax. Lora checked to see if any of Ben got any worse, and asked Bruce to double check the wounds just to be sure of the condition of the injuries. After Bruce told everyone the wounds didn't get any worse, he asked, "Are you doing all right, Ben?"

Ben said in response, "I still feel in a little bit of pain, but I'm still trying to relax."

Bruce then said, "Well, since we finally got you into the shuttle, would anyone like stay here and keep Ben company as well as to take care of him?"

Lora answered with, "I will stay here with Ben and make sure his condition or wounds don't get any worse."

After the others agreed to let Lora stay in the shuttle with Ben to watch over him, they started to go back to the house to find the remaining people of their group who are still some where in the house. Before they got into the house, Steve said, "When we get back inside, I think we should go to the second floor and check out that strange hallway."

Leslie asked, "Why do you think we should check that strange hallway that gives out a certain level of evil intention every time any of us get near the door at the center of it?"

Steve replied with, "Because if we want to actually burn down every part of this house, we have to find out what exactly is giving out that evil sensation."

Everyone thought about what Steve told them for a moment to figure out if he was completely right to find out what the source of the dark sensation in the hallway on the second floor was. When they finally found out Steve had a point, all of them continued their way back into the house. By the time they were all back into the house, everyone began to quickly go to the center of the house, where the stairs to the second floor was at.

A moment later, everyone finally got to the center of the house and were staring at the stairs as if some of them were having second thoughts about what they were to do and where to go next. Bruce looked at everyone and then asked, "Is everyone ready to go up those stairs and find out what exactly is giving out that evil sensation throughout that middle hallway?"

For a moment, most of them thought about what they were going to do in the hallway on the second floor while the rest said they were ready for it. When the others at last said they were set to go, all of them immediately started to go up the stairs. A short while later, everyone were finally on the second floor and were about to be in front of the hallway they were all going to go in.

Once all of them were in front of the hallway, they right away felt the dark and evil sensation like before, but a bit stronger now. Then Steve said, "Well, let's go inside this hallway and find whatever is giving out this strange sensation."

THE HAUNTED HOUSE

After Steve said that, the others nodded to reply that they were ready to go. When they were going through the hallway, all of them felt that the evil sensation was growing as they got deeper into the hallway.

A moment later, everyone noticed they were at the end of the hallway and saw the door that was at the center of it. Marissa then asked, "What should we do now? Should we see what is behind this door?"

Steve answered with, "We should, because this is where the strange sensation we are feeling in this hallway is coming from."

The others thought Steve was right about where the strange sensation was coming from and that it was coming from whatever is behind the door. After everyone agreed to find out what exactly was behind the door, Bruce volunteered to be the one to open it. By the time Bruce got to the door and had a hold of the doorknob, he opened it all the way so the others would be able to see what was behind the door from where they were currently standing.

Everyone saw nothing out of the ordinary, just a room with wooden tables and old lamps. After all of them saw that, everyone started to walk into the room to find out what else was is in the room. When they saw what was inside the room, all of them saw more old furniture that seemed to them to be about a hundred or so years old.

Then one of them noticed something as the far end of the room. Leslie told the others of what she saw at the end of the room. The moment everyone saw what Leslie pointed out to them, they saw a woman sitting in a rocking chair, and she had pale white hair.

Marissa whispered, "Who do you guys think the woman on the rocking chair is?"

Bruce answered with, "I think none of us know who it is, but let's go and find out."

While they were walking toward the woman on the rocking chair, most of them called out to the lady to see if she will answer back to them, while the rest continued to walk to where the lady was at. When the lady never answered back to any of them who did so, they stopped doing that and just walked to her to find out who exactly is the woman in the rocking chair is.

A short while later, everyone were at a distance where they could find out the woman was, but a few of them noticed something that disturbed them and stopped them from getting any closer to the lady.

When Steve saw that on their faces, he asked, "What is the matter, guys? Why do you all have that disturbed look on your faces?"

Leslie responded with, "We saw something about the lady in the rocking chair that has freaked us out by it."

Bruce replied with, "What did you both see about the lady that would freak both of you out?"

Marissa pointed out to the others of what she and Leslie had seen that disturbed them about the woman in the rocking chair.

When the others saw the hands of the lady in rocking chair, they noticed both of them were very thin and dried up, which made them think there might be a possibility the lady might either be very old or dead. After they realized that and understood why Leslie and Marissa were freaked out by it, Steve told them that Bruce and he noticed what they saw about the lady.

Marissa then asked, "What are we going to do next?"

Steve said in response, "We are going to see the woman really is and find out if she is also dead or not."

Leslie followed with, "Are you going to make us along with you guys to do that? Because I think the both of us don't want to go anywhere closer than where we are standing right now."

After Leslie told the others that, they both didn't want to force them to do something that neither of them wanted to do, and with good reason. Then Bruce told them to wait where they were standing until they discovered who the woman in the rocking chair was. By the time Bruce and Steve were standing on both sides of the woman in the rocking chair, they both thoroughly studied the lady to see who she was in reality.

Then after a short moment, Bruce realized who the woman in the rocking chair really was and thought it to be utterly impossible for it to be that person in the end. When Marissa asked Bruce what was wrong as well as what had occurred to him, he answered with, "I just figured out who the woman in rocking chair really was, but it couldn't be her for specific reasons."

Then Leslie asked, "Who is the woman in the rocking chair in the end that you would find it impossible to be that person for whatever obvious reasons?"

Right before Bruce was to answer Leslie's question, Steve quickly responded with, "The woman in the rocking chair is really Elizabeth Griffin."

While Leslie and Marissa were both shocked by what Steve said about who was the woman in the rocking chair in the end, Bruce asked Steve when Steve had figured out it was Elizabeth in the rocking chair.

Steve replied with, "I think I figured it out probably right after you did, as far as I know."

A moment later, Marissa asked, "What made the two of you realize that the woman in rocking chair was actually Elizabeth?"

Bruce answered with, "It was mostly because of what the woman was wearing and the ring she had on the finger that is a sign of being married."

Marissa went to see if what Bruce told them about the woman and had them say that it was Elizabeth. While Marissa was walking to the woman in the rocking chair to find out if it really was Elizabeth Griffin, Leslie was still in fear of getting any closer to the lady in the chair. When Marissa saw Leslie didn't move at all, she asked, "Why aren't you moving like me? Don't you want to see if it really is Elizabeth in the rocking chair?"

Leslie responded with, "I just don't feel like going to see the woman in the chair because even if it really was Elizabeth, that would not change the fact of it possibly being a decaying corpse." After Leslie told her that, Marissa asked the others if Elizabeth was a corpse in the chair. Steve said in response, "I'm sorry, she is a corpse in the chair."

Chapter 8

When Marissa heard that, she looked behind her and saw Leslie looked more frightened than she was before. After seeing that, Marissa told Leslie to stay where she was and to let her check out the woman's appearance to find out if both Bruce and Steve were telling the truth. By the time Marissa finally saw the woman's appearance from the front and discovered it really was Elizabeth's corpse that was in the rocking chair, she told Leslie that the others were telling them the truth about the lady in the chair.

After she told Leslie about who was the corpse in the chair, Marissa asked, "What does that mean if this is Elizabeth's corpse?"

The others thought about it and did so thoroughly so that the moment any of them figured it out, they would tell everyone the answer that would also make sense. A moment later, Steve said, "That would mean that it's Elizabeth who is haunting this house."

Then after Steve said that to the others, Leslie asked, "What makes you say that?"

Steve said, "Because if this is her decaying corpse, then it was her ghost that has been doing all the things to all of us ever since she allowed us to come in and stay until the weather outside got more better than it was at the time."

Marissa then said, "So you are saying that all the events that has occurred to each of us were both caused and controlled by Elizabeth?"

THE HAUNTED HOUSE

Steve replied with, "Yes, that is what I'm saying, and it also means that Elizabeth is the one who killed Earl when he was following her."

The others thought about what Steve told them and see if he had a point about Elizabeth being the one who killed Earl.

Before they agreed to Steve's point, Leslie asked, "So that would mean that Elizabeth is a monster because Earl's apparition told all of us that he was killed by some kind of ferocious creature."

Steve nodded to reply to what Leslie said to all of them. When everyone agreed to what Steve told them about Elizabeth, Marissa asked, "What should we do now, since now we know who is the one that is haunting this house and is also the one that has some kind of control on all of the things that has happened to each of us?"

Bruce then said, "I think that we should burn this room first so we can be able to burn anything that hasn't caught on fire."

After everyone agreed to Bruce's idea, he went to Leslie to try to calm her, for she still seemed to be frozen in fear. The moment Steve and Marissa were out of the room and in the hallway, the door suddenly closed behind them very hard.

Then after the door to the room they were in closed hard behind them, Steve tried to open it but wasn't able to do so because the door wouldn't open even with the doorknob being loose instead of locked. When he found that moving the doorknob was no longer enough to open the door to get Bruce and Leslie out of the room, Steve started to ram against the door to open it.

While Steve was doing that to try to get the others out of the room, Marissa asked, "Hey, are you two all right in there?"

Bruce answered with, "We're doing okay. Are you having trouble opening the door from your side?"

Marissa said in response, "Yeah, we are. You two doing the same on your side?"

Leslie replied with, "Yes, and we aren't able to open it even when we put our strength into doing it."

Then from out of nowhere, Bruce and Leslie began to hear a wail go throughout the room. When they heard that, both of them looked around the room to see where it was coming from. A moment later, Leslie tapped Bruce on the shoulder and said, "I think you might want to see this." The moment Bruce looked at what Leslie wanted him to see, he saw Elizabeth's corpse was no longer in the rocking chair.

Leslie then asked, "Where in the world did Elizabeth's corpse go to?"

Both of them walked to the chair to make sure the corpse was really gone. When Bruce and Leslie were halfway to the chair, both of them heard a familiar voice say, "Hello, you two. How are the both of you doing?"

They both recognized the voice, but neither of them could believe it. Then Bruce and Leslie looked behind them to make sure that it was her without a doubt.

After they saw it was Elizabeth who was the voice they heard, both of them were wondering how that was even possible. Then Elizabeth said, "If you are both wondering how I'm doing this, I think I wouldn't need to explain exactly how I'm doing this."

Leslie replied with, "So you are a ghost that is haunting this house."

Once Elizabeth nodded to answer what Leslie said to her, Bruce asked, "How exactly are you haunting this house?"

Elizabeth made an evil smile and responded with, "Well, I did some things so I would always have this house to myself."

Leslie followed with, "Do any of those things you did to keep the house for yourself involve killing people?"

Elizabeth answered with, "Yes, they did, and I know you two as well as the others have an idea on who those people are."

After Elizabeth said that, Bruce and Leslie both realized what she was telling them. Then Bruce said, "Are you saying you killed all those people in the portraits we all found?"

Elizabeth nodded to answer Bruce's question.

Leslie then asked, "Including the little boy we saw in one of the portraits?"

Elizabeth said in response, "No, I would never hurt nor kill the only child I ever had when I was still alive."

THE HAUNTED HOUSE

After Elizabeth told them that she didn't do any kind of harm to the boy, Bruce asked, "So exactly why did you kill all those other people while you were still somewhat human?"

Elizabeth giggled for a short moment and replied with, "That is an easy question to answer. To get every single thing they had and see what was worth keeping or to sell to specific groups of people."

When Bruce and Leslie heard Elizabeth's response about why she killed those people, they thought she was what both of them and probably everyone else in the group would call a black widow murderer to the rich.

A moment later, Elizabeth asked, "Would either of you two be interested in knowing how this whole me killing people and haunting this entire house happened?"

Bruce and Leslie told Elizabeth they were interested in the information she was going to tell them.

Then Elizabeth said, "Around the time I got married to James, I was unhappy living with him because he would always order me to do chores or any other kind of work, even though we had maids to do that while I do what a wife was supposed to do those days."

Elizabeth went on to tell them how her husband always mistreated her every single day, which made her irritated as well as angry by the way she was living with him. Then a moment later, Elizabeth continued with, "In 1817, I caught him kissing one of the maids in the kitchen, which made me utterly furious by it."

Elizabeth then went on to tell them that after seeing her husband do the same thing with the same maid several times, she got to the breaking point where she began to think evil and demented things to do to them. Elizabeth then said, "After a few weeks, I finally had the courage to what I felt like doing to them, and that was to murder both of them."

The moment Elizabeth got to the point of her story where she tells them how she murdered her husband and the maid, they thought it was brutal the way she killed them and what she used to do so. Elizabeth told them she killed James and the maid with an ax from the shed in the garden and showed the two no mercy or hesitation.

Elizabeth followed with saying she had their bodies buried in a part of the garden no one else but her would know, since she was the only one that ever went into the garden. After she finished burying the remains, she cleaned up and went to the living room to think about what she had done to her husband and the maid.

She thought what she did was right, even though not everyone might do exactly what she did to them, but she later on found another good thing for her killing James. Elizabeth discovered she would be able to have as well as get all of James's belongings and everything else he ever had, especially those that were worth a small fortune if they were ever sold.

Then Leslie asked, "Did anyone ever question you where your husband or even the maid was?"

Elizabeth answered with, "Not that much people asked for his whereabouts, but whenever anybody did, I told them that he left me without saying as well as the maid without a reason to do so probably around the same time."

Elizabeth then told them after she discovered and was never found for her husband's sudden disappearance, she began to have thoughts and/or plans to get married again to another wealthy man and do the same thing to him so she would get all their worthy belongings. She went on telling them she killed all those people for their property, and did so even when she had a child.

After Elizabeth said that, Bruce asked, "Did you kill the father of your child before he was born?"

Elizabeth shook her head and replied with, "Regretfully, I didn't, because during the time I was with the child, my mind and complete thoughts were in a state that others knew was normal for mothers to be."

Then Leslie asked, "What happened after you delivered the boy?"

Elizabeth said in response, "I allowed the father of my son to live so we can raise the child together."

Bruce and Leslie were both puzzled by Elizabeth letting her son's father live to raise the boy together. Elizabeth then said, "Just to let the two of you know if you are wondering why I let the father live

THE HAUNTED HOUSE

to raise my son with me, it was because my mental state was still in motherly love and care instead of how it was before I was with child."

Bruce and Leslie realized what previous state of mind Elizabeth was referring to. The moment they knew what Elizabeth was telling them about, Leslie asked, "When did your state of mind go back to the way it was before having your son?"

Elizabeth answered with, "It was around the time my son was turning fifteen years old, and I immediately began to have ideas to kill his father in a way my son doesn't think it was caused by someone."

Elizabeth went to tell Bruce and Leslie that a few days after her son officially turned fifteen, she had a plan to kill the father and to make it appear like it was an accident, which seemed easy for her with the many things and places to do the deed. In the end, Elizabeth used the second floor to kill him, and did so when she saw the chance to execute her plan.

Elizabeth finally killed her husband by shoving him over to fall hard to the first floor. She had a big evil smile when she saw his body broken on the floor. By the time Elizabeth got her sights off her husband's dead body, she was utterly shocked to see her son standing a few feet from the body of his father with a scared look on his face.

When he and Elizabeth caught each other's sight, the boy said, "Why did you kill Dad? What did he do that made you want to push him off from up there on the second floor?" Elizabeth denied she had pushed him over and told her son that he fell over because he tripped over his feet. The boy shouted that she was lying because he saw everything from the beginning, and then quickly started to run to his room, which was in the hallway in front of the stairs.

Chapter 9

A short while later, Elizabeth got to the door to her son's room and right away began to knock on the door as well as asking him to open the door so she can explain things face to face. When he didn't open the door or answer Elizabeth, she went through the keys of the house to find the one to her son's door and unlocked it to get inside.

The moment Elizabeth finally found the key to the door, she immediately put it in the keyhole and turned it to the left to unlock it. When Elizabeth got the door unlocked and went inside the room, she saw that a few cabinet drawers were open and the window open. Elizabeth didn't see her son the moment she entered the room.

Elizabeth immediately checked every part of the room to see if he was still in the room or if he actually went outside through the window. While checking the room for her son, Elizabeth noticed there were several clothes missing in each of the cabinet drawers. Then Elizabeth realized what that would mean and quickly went toward the closet to find if what she was looking for was still in there.

By the time she didn't see a traveling bag his father gave him for whenever they went somewhere for vacation or fun, Elizabeth went to the window and looked outside to see if he was still nearby. A moment later, Elizabeth finally caught sight of her son, who was already halfway down the road as well as running as fast as he could. Elizabeth shouted out to him and told him to come back home, but he didn't reply or look back while running down the road.

THE HAUNTED HOUSE

When Elizabeth lost complete sight of her son, she was utterly distraught by seeing her own son running away from the house, mostly her, and never looking back when she was shouting out to him. A short while later, Elizabeth was in the room they were in right now and sat in the rocking chair, looking outside, still in complete and utter distress for losing her son.

Elizabeth told them she stopped eating and doing everything else because she felt already dead as well as gone in this world the moment she lost her son. It was only a few weeks later she had both officially and utterly died by the way she was living in her last moments in her life. A few years later, Elizabeth came back to this world but as a ghost that haunts the entire house.

It took Elizabeth a week and a half to be able to both possess something in this house. After she was able to do that, Elizabeth waited to see if anyone would stop by her house so she would see how it would feel like to kill people as a ghost. It was only a month later someone came by the house to see how it looked inside instead of the outside.

The moment the man was inside, Elizabeth engulfed him in one of the rooms that was close to the kitchen and killed him fiercely when he was inside. After killing the man, Elizabeth felt better about killing people than when she was still alive. Elizabeth patiently waited for the next person or people to stop by the house to repeat what she did to the man, but in whatever way she choose to do so.

People came by the house every once in a while for many reasons, but most of them were to check the house from the inside. Elizabeth tells Bruce and Leslie that the last person to come by the house was about forty years ago, until the group came along due to their tire dilemma as well as the way the weather was when they came to her house to ask if they could until it got more better.

By the time Elizabeth finished telling her story as well as the moment she became the ghost that haunts the entire house and what she did as the ghost of the house, Leslie asked, "Did you ever see or find anything about your son at all?"

Elizabeth shook he head and said, "I would have to say that I never did find my son or see him as well."

Bruce then asked, "What was your son's name? Because with all the things you have here, you could have gotten someone to find where he was and what he was doing in his life."

Elizabeth replied with, "I did hire an investigator to tell me where he was and what name was he using."

Leslie then said, "And did your investigator find out the information you wanted to know?"

Elizabeth answered with, "The investigator found where he was for a short time and the name he was using, which made me feel even more depressed than I was before."

Then Bruce asked, "Where was he living, and what was the name he was using that made you more sad than ever?"

Elizabeth said in response, "He was living in a small town close by but then moved somewhere else without leaving a forwarding address, and was using his father's last name, which sickened me with both knowing and finding it out."

Then Leslie said, "What was his father's last name that your son was using instead of yours?"

Elizabeth answered with, "His father's last name was Knightly."

After Elizabeth said that, Leslie looked at Bruce and saw he looked like he was both surprised and shocked by what she said. Bruce then asked, "What was your son's full name when he was using his father's last name?"

Elizabeth replied with, "His name was Henry B. Knightly."

The moment Elizabeth told them that, Bruce started to slowly step back and then said, "That can't be, that's impossible."

When Leslie heard what Bruce said, she asked, "What's wrong, Bruce? Did something Elizabeth said startle you?" After she saw Bruce nod his head to answer her question, Leslie said, "What did Elizabeth say that would startle you?"

Bruce said in response, "The name of Elizabeth's son."

Leslie followed with, "What about the name of Elizabeth's son? Is it the name of someone you know?"

Then Bruce asked Elizabeth, "Was your son's name Bartholomew?"

Elizabeth had a surprised look on her face, which Bruce and Leslie noticed as well, and said, "Yes, it was. How did you know that?"

After Elizabeth said that, Bruce responded with, "Because Henry Bartholomew Knightly was my grandfather."

The moment Bruce said that, both Leslie and Elizabeth were both shocked by it. A moment later, Leslie said, "So you are in a way related to Elizabeth because of your grandfather?"

Bruce nodded and said, "Regretfully, I have to say that I am related to Elizabeth by my grandfather."

Then Elizabeth asked, "Is my son still alive or not?"

Bruce replied with, "I would have to say no. My grandfather died in a car accident a few years ago."

The moment Elizabeth heard that, she appeared to be saddened by what Bruce said. Elizabeth then said, "Well, I guess I have to make sure that you never leave this house and to have all your friends in a special way."

Bruce and Leslie looked at each other, wondering what she was trying to say with that last comment. Leslie then asked, "What do you mean by killing Bruce's friends in a special way? Do you have something already planned for us?"

Elizabeth smirked and replied with, "I did the moment I got you in here, but now I have made some easy adjustments to it."

After Elizabeth said that to Bruce and Leslie, she laughed evilly for a moment and then disappeared. When Elizabeth disappeared from their sights and they couldn't see her anywhere else in the room, the door suddenly opened and let Steve and Marissa in the room. After they were in the room with Bruce and Leslie, Marissa asked, "What happened to you guys? Why did the two of you stop trying to get this door open?"

When Marissa said that, Bruce and Leslie were both surprised to know neither of them heard Elizabeth inside the room or what she told the both of them. After they realized that, Leslie said, "We had a very strange encounter with Elizabeth when we were trapped inside this room."

Steve said in response, "But that is impossible. We all saw her corpse in this room."

Leslie replied with, "We know that, but the Elizabeth we had the encounter with wasn't her corpse but her apparition."

Bruce followed with, "And she told us what she did when she was alive and her time as a ghost that haunts this house."

After Leslie and Bruce told the others of what they experienced in the room, Marissa asked, "Did she ever tell you about the portraits?"

Leslie said in response, "Yes, she did, and it was quite the story she told us about each of them, especially the one with the little boy."

Steve then asked, "Why did she have so many portraits of her with different men?"

Bruce replied with, "For Elizabeth, it was some kind of way for her to remember all those that came after her first man in her life."

After Bruce said that, Marissa responded with, "Were each of those men husbands that came after James, her first husband?"

Leslie answered with, "Yes they were. Also, all of them died for the same reason."

Then Steve asked, "And what was the reason all of those men in the portraits you two and the others found in different places on the first floor?"

Bruce said in response, "For Elizabeth to be able to get all of their belongings and items that had some what of a great value if she were to ever sell any of them."

When Steve and Marissa heard that, they thought that made Elizabeth into some kind of gold-digging serial killer who has become a murderous and powerful ghost that is haunting the house.

A moment later, Steve asked, "And the boy from one of the portraits, what happened to him?"

Marissa followed with, "Did Elizabeth do any kind of harm to him?"

Leslie replied with, "The only kind of harm or damage Elizabeth ever did to the boy was mostly mental scarring." After Leslie told the others that, Steve then asked, "What exactly do you mean by that? How did Elizabeth mentally scar the boy?"

Bruce answered with, "By accidentally having the boy watch her kill his own father, which he didn't take it very well as expected from watching that kind of scene happen before your very eyes."

THE HAUNTED HOUSE

When Steve and Marissa heard what Bruce told them of how Elizabeth mentally scarred her son, they wondered what the boy did after watching his father be killed by his own mother.

Before asking Bruce and Leslie anything else, Marissa said, "How did Elizabeth kill the boy's father that he witnessed happen right in front of him?"

Leslie responded with, "Elizabeth killed the boy's father by pushing him off the second floor. He landed hard on the ground of the first floor."

After Leslie said that, Steve and Marissa imagined what the boy had witnessed and realized that could be a scarring moment for him that will be hard to forget.

Chapter 10

Then when they found out how the boy's father was killed and how the boy could have felt at that moment, Steve asked, "What did the boy do after witnessing that horrible event?"

Bruce answered with, "He despised his mother so much that he ran to his room and got a travel bag that he filled with some of his clothes."

Leslie followed with, "He then went through the window he had in his room and quickly ran away from this house."

After Leslie said that, Marissa asked, "And what did Elizabeth do after her son ran away from her and the house?."

Leslie replied with, "Elizabeth closed herself in this room we're standing in right now until she finally died."

Steve then said, "So she later became a ghost that is haunting the entire house. Did she ever find any information about her son's whereabouts?"

Bruce said in response, "Well, you're right about her being the ghost haunting the whole house, and she did find some information about her son."

When they heard that, Marissa asked, "When did Elizabeth find information about her son?"

Leslie replied with, "Elizabeth never told us when exactly she found that information, but I would have to guess it was right before she died."

THE HAUNTED HOUSE

Steve then said, "What was the information Elizabeth found about her son?"

Bruce answered with, "Elizabeth found out where was he was living at for a short amount of time and the name he was using."

Then after Steve and Marissa heard that, they asked Bruce what was the name her son was using. Bruce looked at Marissa and Steve, hesitating to tell them what they wanted to know. The moment Leslie noticed that, she said, "His name is something that relates both closely and personally to Bruce that it utterly shocked him when he found out."

Steve then asked, "What was the son's name that it would relate to Bruce in such a way?"

A short moment later, Bruce said in response, "His name was Henry B. Knightly, and he was my grandfather."

When Steve and Marissa heard that, they showed the same expression on their faces like Bruce had when he heard the name of his grandfather from Elizabeth and also when he found out he was her son as well.

Then Marissa asked, "Are you completely sure that Elizabeth was telling the both of you the truth?"

Leslie replied with, "Yes, she was, because Bruce asked Elizabeth about her son's middle name to make sure of his suspicions about it were true."

Steve followed with, "And what was Elizabeth's son middle name that made the both of you say it was Bruce's grandfather?"

Bruce answered with, "It was Bartholomew. I can also say that, without a single shred of doubt, it was him."

Steve said in response, "Exactly how can you prove that?"

Bruce replied with, "My grandfather's date of birth and the date of the portrait he was in with Elizabeth and his father."

After Bruce told the others that, Marissa asked, "How can those things prove that Elizabeth's son was your grandfather?"

Bruce replied with, "Well, with his date of birth, the date on the portrait, and the age Elizabeth told us her son had around the time he ran away prove that it was my grandfather without a doubt."

The moment Marissa and Steve heard that, they figure if Bruce did his math on those variables, then he was completely and utterly telling them the truth about Elizabeth's son being his own grandfather.

Then Marissa said, "And what happened after you figured all that out?"

Bruce once again hesitated in telling Steve and Marissa what they wanted to know, so Leslie replied with, "Bruce freaked out in a certain way that he accidentally said it out loud that Elizabeth's very son was his grandfather."

Steve and Marissa were both showing expressions of surprise and wonder on their faces.

When the others saw that, Bruce and Leslie knew that neither of them would have to guess why they would have those expressions after hearing what she told them.

Steve then asked, "What happened after Bruce unknowingly did that?"

Leslie answered with, "Elizabeth told us that she was not going to allow Bruce any kind of escape from this house, and that she also came up with a special way to kill the rest of us off, which surprised me a lot."

Marissa then asked, "Did Elizabeth ever tell you in what way she was going to kill us?"

Leslie answered with, "I asked her, and she said that she already had something planned for all of us, but after finding out that Bruce was related to her son, Elizabeth told us that she immediately improved as well as made some changes to her plans."

Bruce followed with, "After Elizabeth told us that, she laughed evilly as well as disappeared from our sights and we didn't see her any in the room anymore."

After the others heard that, Steve asked, "What should we do now with all the things we know and found out now?"

Then Leslie replied with, "I think we should continue with looking for John and Sarah so we can finally finish burning this house down before Elizabeth comes back and does whatever she has planned for all of us, except Bruce."

THE HAUNTED HOUSE

After Steve and Marissa heard that, they agreed to do Leslie's plan. A moment later, right before they were about to go outside and do Leslie's plan to look for the remaining members of the group, all of them heard a couple of thumping noises coming from somewhere to their right. Once all of them heard those noises, they looked to all the places that were to their right and found out where the noises came from.

When Bruce saw a door to what he thought could be some kind of closet, he began to walk toward it to find out if the thumping noises came from there. The moment the others saw him move forward for some reason, Steve asked, "Hey, Bruce, what are you doing?"

Marissa followed with, "Where are you going to?"

Bruce pointed ahead of him and said in response, "I think the noises we heard came from behind that door."

When they saw the door Bruce was telling them about, all of them thought he might have a point of where the noises might have came from. Marissa then asked, "What makes you think that the noises came from that door?"

Then Bruce answered with, "Because out of all of the places that we heard the noises come from, that is the only place I believe the noises could have come from."

Everyone thought about what Bruce told them thoroughly to make sure he was telling the truth. The moment everyone found out Bruce was telling them the truth, they started to walk as well as catch up to where Bruce was at.

When they finally caught up to where Bruce was at, all of them were at the door and waited for Bruce to open it to see what was behind it. By the time he got the door unlocked and slowly opened it, the others saw an arm, which startled some of them. After Bruce and the others saw that, he opened the door quickly to find out who that arm belonged to or if it was still attached to a person.

The moment Bruce got the door all the way open, they were shocked by what all of them found as well as saw what was behind the door and who that arm belonged to. Everyone saw the arm belonged to John, and beside him was Sarah. Another thing they saw was they were both unconscious. Other than that, all of them also saw that both Sarah and John appeared to have been through something quite possibly rough as well as fierce.

Their clothes were torn and ripped in several places, as if they had been attacked and or mauled by an animal. After they realized that about the condition of both Sarah's and John's clothes, some of them started to try and wake them up from their sleep. A moment later, Sarah and John were finally awake, as well as beginning to stand up on their feet.

When John cleared his sight, he was glad to see the others. But when Sarah cleared her sight, she jumped back and shrieked all of a sudden. Marissa then asked, "What's wrong, Sarah, why did you scream all of a sudden?"

Sarah answered with, "I saw Elizabeth, and that was the reason why I screamed."

After Sarah said that, Steve asked, "Where did you see Elizabeth?"

Sarah replied with, "I saw her a few feet behind all of you, and she had an evil smile on her face that almost seemed somewhat demented."

When the others heard that, they all looked behind them to see if Elizabeth was still there where Sarah told them. The moment they didn't see her behind them, Bruce asked, "Other than the smile, how did Elizabeth appear to you?"

Leslie followed with, "Did Elizabeth have pale hair that was as white as snow?"

When Sarah heard what Leslie asked, she was surprised, and wondered why she would ask her that very precise description of Elizabeth's hair. Sarah then asked, "She did have pale white hair and pale skin as well. How did you know that?"

The moment Sarah confirmed what Leslie wanted to know about Elizabeth's appearance, she and the others looked at each other, realizing as well as knowing what it meant if Elizabeth showed up like that and Sarah was the only one that saw it.

Sarah then asked, "What is it? Why did all of you look at one another just now?"

John followed with, "I was wondering the same thing. Does it have to do with how Sarah saw Elizabeth appear to her?"

Bruce answered with, "Yes, it does, because if Elizabeth appeared to Sarah in that form—"

Leslie continued with, "That means Elizabeth is the form of how she ended up looking like as a corpse."

Chapter 11

After Leslie told Sarah and John that, they were both shocked when they heard her say "Elizabeth's corpse." Then Sarah asked, "Are you saying that Elizabeth is actually dead and has been that way before we came into her house?"

Everyone nodded in answer to Sarah's question to them. John then said, "If that is so, how did you all find out that she was actually dead?"

Steve said in response, "We all found her corpse here in this room, and it appeared to have been dead for quite a long time."

After Sarah and John heard what Steve told them how they found out that Elizabeth was really dead all this time, they were both surprised by finding out that Elizabeth was never alive and hasn't been for some time now.

When Sarah and John were caught up with what has occurred and what the others have discovered, they wanted to know what all of them should do now. Steve answered with, "Well, since we have found you two, I think all we have left to do is burn the entire floor down."

Sarah then asked, "Why would you want to burn the entire second floor?."

John followed with, "Did all of you have difficulty burning a hallway or something?"

Bruce replied with, "We all found out that the hallway that lead to this room could never, no matter what we tried to do, catch on fire."

After Bruce told Sarah and John that, they thought that it couldn't be possible but then remembered whenever any of them got close to the hallway, all of them would feel something eerie and evil go through it.

After they remembered that, John said, "Well then, where should we start to burn this entire floor?"

Steve responded with, "We should all start from this room, because if we started from the outside, there might be a chance that it won't catch on fire."

When Steve pointed that out to the others, all of them knew he was right to start from inside the room so it can catch on fire and then progressively burn everything on the second floor.

A moment later, after Sarah and John took a few steps out of the closet they were both in, both of them suddenly fell to the floor hard. When Sarah and John were lying down on the floor, they were both writhing in pain and agony. By the time the others were standing around both Sarah and John, some checked to see why they were in such pain and agony all of a sudden.

When they found out what was the cause of Sarah and John's suffering, Steve said, "We found what is making you both be in such pain."

Sarah then asked, "What is it?"

John followed with, "What is making us feel this much pain and suffering?"

Steve answered with, "It appears that both of you are covered with cuts and bruises. Although the cuts seem minor, the bruises aren't."

After Steve told Sarah and John that, they were both surprised by it. Bruce then asked, "Do either of you know who gave you these cuts and bruises?"

Sarah and John both tried to remember if they know who or what gave them the injuries both of them were suffering from right now. When Sarah remembered the person or thing that gave her and

John the injuries, she hesitated to tell everyone, and they noticed that, which made them wonder why she was hesitating in telling them what they wanted to know.

Then Marissa asked, "What is it, Sarah? Why do you have that look on your face?"

Sarah looked at Marissa, surprised by what she said, and then looked at the others to see if they noticed it as well. After Sarah saw the others had also noticed the look she had on her face, she said, "I think I might know who did this to us, but—"

Steve said in response, "But what? Are you having problems trying to remember who exactly gave the two of you those injuries?"

Sarah answered with, "When I try to remember who gave us these injuries, I just get glimpses of that moment, although I did get a look of the person's face who had caused this suffering to the both of us, but I'm trying to get a clear sight of it right now."

A moment later, Sarah said, "I finally got it, I know who did this to us."

Marissa then asked, "Who was it that gave you two those injuries?"

Sarah replied with, "It was Elizabeth who gave us these injuries, and she did it somewhere very dark."

After Sarah told the others that, John asked, "How is it that you remember most of what happened to us and who did this to us but I can't?"

Sarah said in response, "I don't know exactly why that is. Probably best not to think about it though, because you might not like what it is you can't remember about that moment."

When Sarah said that to John, he thought about it and realized she might be right about him being unable to remember what occurred during the time both of them were getting the injuries they have now by none other than Elizabeth.

After realizing that, John asked, "Do you think we can still walk even with these injuries or not?"

Sarah answered with, "I don't know if we can still walk. Do you want to find out if we are still able to?"

John nodded in response to Sarah's question. The moment they were on their feet, both Sarah and John couldn't stay that long up because it seemed their legs go completely numb and or dead every time they tried to stand up.

By the time both Sarah and John stopped trying to stand up on their feet after several failing attempts to do so, Marissa asked, "Would you both like some help getting up on your feet and getting out of this room to do what has to be done?"

Sarah and John told the others they could get them up to their feet and getting out of the room to then burn the entire second floor.

A moment later, when a couple of the others got Sarah and John to their feet, they started to walk out of the room as quickly as they could. When most of them were out of the room, Bruce suddenly began to hear a voice from out of nowhere and tried to find out where it was coming from. The moment Bruce couldn't find where the voice he was hearing was coming from, he then realized it was coming from within his head.

After he realized where the voice was coming from, Bruce tried to then figure out who was the person who was talking to him from his mind. A moment later, Leslie asked, "Hey, Bruce, what's the matter? Why did you stop?"

Bruce didn't listen to what Leslie said to him but instead tried to keep his focus on whose was the voice he was hearing.

By the time Bruce finally figured out whose was the voice he was hearing, he was both shocked and surprised to find out it was Elizabeth who was talking to him. While Bruce was hearing Elizabeth talking to him from his mind, all she kept saying to him was his name. Then after he found out that it was Elizabeth who was the voice he was hearing in his head, Bruce said, "What do you want? Why are you talking to me?"

When Bruce said to no one, Leslie replied with, "Bruce, who are you talking to? Because as far as we can see, you are talking to nobody."

Bruce looked at Leslie and the others to see how worried they were about him talking to no one in the room. The moment he noticed their faces, Bruce said, "I'm sorry. It's just that I began to hear a voice from out of nowhere, but now I know I have stopped hearing it."

After Bruce said that to the others, Leslie asked, "Well, if you have stopped hearing that voice, would you like to come along with us now?"

Bruce nodded and replied with, "Sure, let's continue our way down the stairs to get the amount of wine bottles we need to burn this floor down."

A moment later, just as Bruce was to be out of the room, the door suddenly closed in front of him. When Bruce got to the door, he immediately tried to get it open but wasn't able to do so, for it seemed the doorknob wouldn't budge even an inch. After he discovered that about the doorknob, Bruce said, "Hey, everyone! I'm locked in this room, and I can't move the doorknob even an inch."

When the others heard what Bruce said, Leslie tried to see if she could open it from her side of the door. The moment she found out she couldn't move the doorknob either, Leslie responded with, "I'm sorry, Bruce, but I can't move the doorknob too."

After Leslie told Bruce that, he replied with, "It's okay, Leslie. I will try to see if I can open it by—"

Right then, at that moment, Bruce started to hear Elizabeth's voice again. Then after that started to happen to him once more, Bruce tried to ignore Elizabeth's voice so as to avoid saying something that might worry the others even more. A moment later, Elizabeth's voice said, "Bruce, look behind you."

After Bruce heard that, he was frightened to look behind him because there might be a chance that Elizabeth would be there. Once he got the courage to look behind him, Bruce did that and was utterly shocked by what he saw. Bruce saw Elizabeth, and he also noticed she had a very demented smile on her face. Bruce then asked, "What do you want, Elizabeth?"

Elizabeth giggled and replied with, "As if you don't already know what I want."

After Elizabeth told him that, Bruce realized what Elizabeth wanted was him. The moment he realized what Elizabeth wanted, Bruce asked, "And what about my friends? Exactly what kind of way are you going to kill them that you consider special?"

THE HAUNTED HOUSE

Elizabeth answered with, "Well, let me just tell you that it involves me taking over someone's entire body and use that person to kill all your friends."

Bruce said in response, "Whose body are you going to take over to kill all my friends?"

After Bruce said that, Elizabeth kept looking at him as well as having an evil and demented smile on her face. Then after he noticed those things from Elizabeth, Bruce immediately realized whom the person she was going to completely control their body to kill all his friends was.

When he found out about whose body Elizabeth was going to possess, Bruce began to quickly try to do whatever he could to try and open the door. While he was doing that, Bruce shouted as well as told the others to get away from the door and to go down to the kitchen to make more combustible wine bottles, or whatever is needed to either burn the house or destroy it completely.

Leslie then asked, "Why do you want us all to get down the stairs and just leave you in that room?"

Bruce answered with, "I just discovered what was the special way Elizabeth has planned to kill all of you, and it scares me a lot."

After Bruce told Leslie and the others that, Marissa asked, "What is it?"

Leslie followed with, "What is Elizabeth's special way to kill us that it would scare you so much?"

Bruce took a moment and then said in response, "By possessing one of us to do so."

When the others heard that, they were shocked by it, and wondered whom Elizabeth would possess to kill everyone but Bruce. Then Leslie said, "Did you find out who Elizabeth is going to possess?"

Bruce replied with, "Yes, I did. And this is the part that frightens me the most because after I found out who it was going to be, I had to get all of you away from here and find a way to burn everything on this floor. That includes the room I'm currently trapped in."

Chapter 12

When the others listened to what Bruce was telling them, they realized who the person Elizabeth was going to possess so she could kill them, as she told them before. Leslie then asked, "Are you telling us that the person Elizabeth is going to possess to kill us is you?"

Bruce answered with, "I have to regretfully say yes. I'm the one Elizabeth is going to take over completely to go on and kill everyone."

Marissa replied with, "And when Elizabeth finishes doing that, she will make sure that you never leave the house and stay with her forever."

After Marissa said that, Bruce said in response, "Exactly, which is the reason why it scares me that if she possesses my body, I think I won't be able to do anything about it at all."

Elizabeth then said, "How right you are, Bruce. And once I have taken complete control over your body, I'm thinking of letting you watch while I kill all of your friends inside this house and the two that are waiting for everyone in the shuttle bus."

When everyone heard Elizabeth say that she was also going to kill Ben and Lora who are in the shuttle bus waiting for them, Bruce asked, "How did you know that there are people in the shuttle bus waiting for us?"

Elizabeth answered with, "Well, I don't know if you have already forgotten. But I told you and the friend that was with you when I told the both of you that I control everything that is inside the house as the grounds that surrounds the house."

Then after Elizabeth told Bruce that, he asked "So you were in control of not just that cloud of smoke that tried to kill me and my friends in the hallway on the first floor, you were also in control of the roots that my friends in the garden and the grounds in front of the house dealt with?"

Elizabeth giggled and replied with, "Well, but of course it was me, and I have to say, Bruce, your friends were lucky in those moments when I attacked them with the roots."

Bruce then asked, "Why do you say that?"

Elizabeth answered with, "Because if it weren't for the ax your friends had in those moments and them resisting from being taken to somewhere unknown to them, they would all be dead." A moment later, Elizabeth said, "Now then, I think it's about time that I get on with taking over your body completely and then killing every single one of your friends."

After Elizabeth told Bruce that, he right away tried to desperately get the door open in any way he could. While Bruce tried to get the door open in whatever way he came up with from his side, everyone else did the same from their side.

A short time later, Bruce said, "Come on, door please open up for goodness' sake." After he said that, Bruce started to hear a loud wail go through the room. When Bruce looked behind him, he saw Elizabeth soaring toward him, and she was in the form of her dead body as well. After he saw that, Bruce shouted to the others, "Forget about me, just get away from this accursed house and get those that got hurt treated as soon as possible, before they get anymore worse than they are right now!"

Leslie said in response, "No, Bruce! I won't leave you here in this evil house to be Elizabeth's prisoner forever. I won't allow that to happen."

Bruce replied with, "You have to, if you and the others want to live, because I don't have want to watch Elizabeth kill all of you while I'm not able to do anything to prevent that from happening!"

After Bruce told Leslie and the others that, everyone else noticed Leslie was beginning to cry, and they were all wondering why she was crying. Then Leslie said, "I won't leave you here to a lifetime of suffering because I love you, Bruce."

The moment Bruce heard Leslie tell him that, he replied with, "If you truly love me, you would go with the others and get far away from this accursed place before—"

At that moment, Leslie felt a loud and vicious thump go through the door. Leslie then asked, "Bruce, what was that loud thump that went through the door?" After she didn't hear an answer or reply from him, she worried that Elizabeth might have begun to gain control over his body. Leslie went on to say, "Are you still there, Bruce?"

Then after Leslie said that, there was a sudden thump that went through the door and was followed by a loud scream that sounded like that of both pain and extreme agony. After the others heard the screams, they immediately realized the screams could only come from Bruce and no one else. Then Leslie said, "What is happening, Bruce? Why are you screaming in such pain and agony?"

Bruce said in response, "I'm trying to fight off Elizabeth from possessing my body completely."

Then after Bruce told the others that, Leslie asked, "Then you can still tell us why exactly are you screaming in so much pain and agony?"

Bruce answered with, "Because Elizabeth is ripping me apart inside and out, probably to weaken my will to resist her control over my body, but at the moment, I seem to be winni—"

After only being halfway through what he was saying to the others, there was a loud scream and was followed with complete silence. When everyone noticed that, they knew that meant Bruce might have ended up losing his fight against Elizabeth's control of his entire body. After all of them realized Bruce might not have control over his body anymore, Steve said, "Hey, John, are you and Sarah still in a lot of pain the both of you were when we were still in the room?"

John replied with, "For some reason, I'm still pain, but not that much like before. Why do you ask?"

Steve said in response, "Because if Leslie doesn't follow us soon, she will end up being the first victim of Elizabeth's killing spree in Bruce's body, so I have to make sure that doesn't happen to her at all." A moment later, when Steve was standing directly behind Leslie, he said, "We have to go, Leslie, before that door opens and Elizabeth begins to go through her plan to kill every single one of us while having complete control over Bruce's body to do so."

Leslie responded with, "No, I won't move an inch from here, because if Bruce is forever gone for me, I would rather die than leave this place." After Leslie told Steve that, he said in response, "Well, if that's the case, then you leave me with no other choice."

Before Leslie could ask him what he meant b that, Steve lifted her off her feet and carried her on his shoulders.

While Leslie was fighting as well as telling Steve to put her down and leave her here, they heard a creaking sound from behind them. The moment they saw the doorknob was slowly moving, Steve ran and said, "Quick, everybody, get down the stairs and head towards the front door." By the time most of them were going down the stairs, the door finally opened. Only two of them were there to see it happen.

After Steve saw the door open, he got Leslie off his shoulder so she can get a good sight of what comes out of the room. A short moment later, Bruce came of the room with a smile on his face as well as looking down on the floor for some reason. Then Leslie asked, "Bruce, are you still with us?"

Bruce looked up to get his sights on both Leslie and Steve. Once he got them in his sights, Bruce said in response, "Yes, I am still with you, but just for a moment. Because, after all, I did plan on killing you and everyone else."

When Leslie and Steve heard Bruce tell them that, they noticed the center of his eyes both turned crimson red for a moment. After they both noticed that about Bruce's eyes, Leslie and Steve realized it wasn't Bruce who was before them but Elizabeth, and she appeared to have complete control of his body.

The moment both of them knew that, Leslie and Steve quickly went down the stairs to get as far away from the reach of Elizabeth as they could to avoid getting killed by the hands of Bruce himself. A moment later, Leslie and Steve were finally on the first floor, and saw that John was standing in front of the kitchen for some reason.

When they saw that, Steve asked, "Why are you here instead of being with the others?"

John answered with, "Because even if I went with the others, we would wait for you two and not know if Elizabeth already killed both of you or not."

Leslie then asked, "And why are you standing in front of the kitchen exactly?"

John replied with, "I think I have an idea that might destroy the house completely, but might also kill and destroy Bruce in the process. I'm very sorry, Leslie, if that happens."

After John told the others that, especially Leslie, she seemed to be saddened about his plan having a possibility of both killing as well as destroying Bruce, but then she realized he would want that instead of being a prisoner of Elizabeth forever. The moment she realized that, Leslie then said, "So what exactly is your plan that would destroy this house, and possibly even Bruce along with it?"

John replied with, "We get a few wine bottles to make a streak of wine starting from the kitchen to halfway towards the front door, and then one of us lights it up with a match."

Steve then asked, "And how is that going to destroy this house, and maybe even Bruce?"

John said in response, "Because we are going to use all the gas from the stove so that by the time Bruce gets down here to this floor, there would be enough gas to explode and destroy the house completely."

Then after John said that to Leslie and Steve, they thought that his plan to destroy the house might work even if it will cost them the life of their friend Bruce. A moment later, Steve asked, "Who do you want to help with opening all the lines on the stove, and who will make the streak of wine from inside there to where you want it from the front door, as well as light it when everything is set to do so?"

John then answered with, "Well, I would like you to help me out with the stove while Leslie does the streak of wine from the inside

THE HAUNTED HOUSE

the kitchen to there and light it when everything is ready, if the two of you agree with that."

After John told the others that, they thought about it for a short moment and then nodded their heads to respond to John's question to them.

A moment later, Steve and John were starting to open all the gas lines that were on the stove, while Leslie was opening one of the few wine bottles she got to make the streak from inside the kitchen to where John wanted it to end from the front door. When Steve and John finished opening the gas lines on the stove, they went outside the kitchen to find out how Leslie was doing with the streak of wine.

After Steve and John saw that Leslie was on her last wine bottle as well as almost to where John wanted the streak to end, they smiled but then it immediately disappeared when both of them saw something that scared as well as worried them. The reason being for that was because neither of them knew if there was enough gas throughout the places around them.

Other than not knowing if there was enough gas to destroy the house, they were frightened by the sight of seeing Bruce in front of the second-floor stairs. After they saw Bruce was in front of the stairs on the second floor, he started to slowly come down the stairs. When Steve and John noticed that, they thought he was either mocking them or giving them some time to do whatever they wanted to do before Elizabeth went on to using Bruce's body to kill them and those who were outside in the shuttle bus.

Then a short moment later, Steve and John saw Leslie had finally finished the wine streak to where John wanted to end, which made both of them relieved to know that. After they were relieved with knowing that Leslie had finished the streak of wine, Steve asked, "What should we do now?"

John looked at the progress Bruce had on the stairs and then at Leslie for some apparent reason.

Chapter 13

After he finished doing both, John began to think about what to do next so Steve could get an answer to his question to him. The moment John finally came up with something to follow up with Leslie finishing the wine streak, he said, "Here, take this matchbox that has a few sticks left inside to Leslie so she can light the streak when the moment comes."

When John told him that, Steve then asked, "And what do you want me to do?"

John answered with, "I want you to be with Leslie until she lights up the wine streak, and after that happens, both of you get out of the house before it explodes."

After John said that to Steve, he was surprised to not hear John ever mention himself in his idea and or plan at all. The moment he noticed that, Steve said in response, "What exactly are you going to be doing in those moments?"

John replied with, "I'm going to keep Bruce preoccupied until the moment Leslie lights up the wine streak."

When he heard that, Steve was completely shocked by what John had planned for himself. Then Steve asked, "Do you realize that if you keep Bruce busy, there is a huge chance that you might end up being Elizabeth's first victim on her killing spree while possessing Bruce's body? You know that, right?"

THE HAUNTED HOUSE

John took a moment and then said, "I know, but if I don't do this of keeping Bruce preoccupied and unaware of what we have in stored for him or her to be more precise, she will prevent our plan of action to destroy this house from ever happening, don't you agree?"

After John told that to Steve, Steve thought about it for a moment and found John had a point about what might occur if Elizabeth figured out what they had planned for her. The moment Steve realized that, he said, "And how exactly do you plan on keeping Bruce busy so he doesn't find out anything we have set up to destroy this entire house completely?"

John answered with, "With anyway I come up with that is guaranteed to keep him busy as well as distracted for some time, but enough to get the two of you set to do what the both of you have to do, including what I have told you to go through the moment Leslie lights up the streak of wine."

Steve nodded and responded with, "All right, I'll be sure to tell Leslie your plan and make sure she doesn't do anything to interfere in any way possible."

When Steve said that, John nodded and told him to go on ahead to where Leslie was standing. John also told Steve to tell her about the reason for his plan to keep Bruce preoccupied. Then after Steve agreed to do all the things John told him to do, Steve quickly said his farewell to John and went to where Leslie was standing as well as being careful not to step on the wine streak at all.

After he saw Steve was on his way to Leslie, John looked forward to finding out what Bruce's progress on the stairs was, and was surprised to see Bruce was finally on the first floor. John prepared himself as well as tried to think of a way to distract Bruce from figuring out things he and the others had come up with for him but specifically Elizabeth.

The moment he came up with a way to distract Bruce, John went through with it even though it might seem suicidal to the others and himself. John began to run toward Bruce, even with the pain he was feeling from the injuries he had received from Elizabeth. A moment later, John was close enough to Bruce to be able to throw a punch to his face.

When John landed his punch directly to Bruce's face, he saw Bruce had on a smile, which meant the hit had no effect on him at all. Bruce looked at John with an evil smile on his face and said in a strange voice, "Is that all you have? Because if it is, you have no chance of getting out of this confrontation alive in any way."

John noticed the voice Bruce said those things to him. It was a combination of Bruce's voice and Elizabeth's, which he found quite strange to hear. After noticing that about the sound of Bruce's voice now, John went on to hit him repeatedly in the face to make sure he was wrong about his hits having no effect on Bruce the first time.

A moment later, Bruce finally blocked one of John's punches after receiving several hits from him. Bruce looked at John with a serious look on his face but then made an evil as well as demented smile, bleeding from his mouth while smiling. Bruce cracked his neck and suddenly began to heal all his injuries he had gotten from John's punches to his face.

When John noticed that happening to all of the places he had hit Bruce on the face, he asked, "Why is that happening? How are you healing the injuries I gave you?"

Bruce laughed for a moment and replied with, "Because I won't allow this body to sustain any kind of injury at all."

John realized the voice Bruce had used when he said that to him was none other than Elizabeth's voice.

The moment Bruce was completely healed from all his injuries on his face, he grabbed John by the throat and started to pick him up off his feet. After John was in the air as well as off the floor, he struggled to get himself free from Bruce's grip on his throat. The moment John found out that no matter what he did to get himself loose from Bruce's hold he couldn't, he stopped resisting but then started to kick Bruce anywhere he thought would get him free.

A short moment later, after John kicked Bruce to the side of the head, he got released from his hold. John was relieved to know he was finally free from Bruce's hold on his throat. John tried to catch his breath and treat any kind of injury he could have gotten from the time Bruce had a strong grip on his throat. John wondered why Bruce didn't kill him the moment Bruce had a hold on John by the throat.

After John finished catching his breath, he started to get back on his feet and step a few feet back so Bruce couldn't get another chance to get a hold of him, He might kill John if he does get that opportunity again. When he got back on his feet as well as got out of Bruce's reach, John looked to see if the kick he gave Bruce had more effect than his punches did on him.

When he found out that his kick to the side of Bruce's head didn't have any effect on him either, John shouted in utter disappointment from finding that out. Bruce began to stretch his left arm forward with the hand facing down and pointed his arm in John's direction. John wondered why Bruce was doing that, and wanted to know what he was going to do with his arm stretched out in his direction.

The moment Bruce waved his hand forward toward John, John felt a strong force viciously push him back toward where he was standing, but even more this time because of the forceful push by Bruce's current capabilities since he had been possessed by an evil ghost. The moment John crashed on the wall that was connected to the kitchen, he nearly went through it and broke all the glass that were around the place of the wall he hit.

A moment later, after all the glass fell to the ground around him, John tried to straighten his vision because it appeared blurry for him. By the time John got his vision straightened, he saw there were several cuts on his arms as well as a few on his face and glass shards on the ground around him. After he saw that, John realized how exactly he got all the cuts he now had on his body.

Then John looked forward to see if Bruce was still standing in the same place. John was relieved to know Bruce was still in the same place and was also smiling with the same kind of smile he always showed him and some of the others. To not let Bruce know how he felt of knowing Bruce hasn't moved since he threw him against the kitchen wall, John acted like he was in extreme pain and suffering, which he wasn't that much in either.

When he saw Bruce had bought his little act of physical torment, John staggered to get back up to his feet to continue to keep Bruce focused mostly on him and nothing else, especially Steve and Leslie standing near the front door for a reason he knows, but Bruce didn't and shouldn't find out the reason.

Shortly after John got back to his feet, Bruce asked, "Do you still want more punishment, or should I just finish you off now?"

John said in response, "What is the matter? Are you already bored with me or what?"

Bruce laughed for a moment and replied with, "Well, not exactly, but if you still want more punishment, should I come over to you or you come over to me?"

John thought about it for a moment and looked to the side where the others were standing at near the front door. Then after he knew what he had to do next, John walked toward Bruce so as to keep his focus on him until Leslie decided to light the streak of wine the moment she knew the time to do so was right. When John looked straight at Bruce to see that same evil smile, he then said, "Come on, show me what else you got in store for me."

Bruce said in response, "Well, if that's the case, then let's continue with your punishment as well as torture to your body for causing harm to this body." The moment Bruce said that, John heard only Elizabeth's voice and replied with, "That isn't even your body, Elizabeth. It's my friend Bruce's body, so I think I speak for everyone when I tell you to get out of his body for good."

Bruce laughed with Elizabeth's voice. John noticed the way he laughed was like as if someone just told a really hilarious joke that would make people laugh like that. After Bruce stopped laughing, he then said, "If you or anyone else thinks I will ever let go of this and even allow Bruce to be free from my hold, then all of you are wasting your time as well as your strength, because that will never happen."

After Bruce said that in Elizabeth's voice to John, he was saddened for knowing that, and then realized that Leslie would be even more depressed with that fact of Elizabeth never releasing Bruce from her grasp because she loves him. When he realized that, John contin-

THE HAUNTED HOUSE

ued to go toward Bruce and whatever Elizabeth wanted to give him as punishment.

By the time John was only a few feet away from Bruce, he began to once again hit Bruce but this time in different parts of his body other than his face. John also used his legs to hit Bruce as well and aimed for his legs when he was using them. A moment later, when John got exhausted and stopped hitting Bruce to regain his energy as well as breath, Bruce right away began to heal all his injuries he got from the hits once again. However, this time, John could hear bones crack from all the areas he had hit, including both of Bruce's legs. John realized this time around of hitting Bruce had caused even more damage than he ever expected to have on him.

The moment Bruce finished healing all his injuries, he made a look on his face that seemed as if he wasn't happy anymore, and said, "I know you heard a few bones crack, so allow me to crack one of yours."

After Bruce said that once again in Elizabeth's voice to John, John immediately backed away from Bruce's reach, but for some reason, he stopped moving. John tried to move back some more but found it impossible to do so. He then began to move anything else to see if he was still able to move at all. The moment he realized he was no longer able to move, John asked, "What's happening to me? Why can't I move my arms or legs at all?"

Bruce said in response, "That is because I'm currently not allowing you to do so."

When John heard that, he looked at Bruce to find out how exactly he was making him unable to move anything, John then realized this was the same force Bruce used to push him very hard back toward the kitchen wall. Then after John had realized that, he said, "Are you using the same power you used on me to viciously push me back against the kitchen wall and nearly went through that very same wall?"

When John asked Bruce that, he smiled and answered with, "Well, if you must know, it is, but I choose to only use my left hand this time instead of the whole arm, which seems powerful enough to enable you to move any part of your body even by itself, wouldn't you agree?"

John replied with, "I wouldn't have no other choice but to agree with you on that. What kind of power are you using that is able to be used by Bruce as well?"

Bruce said in response, "Your friend Bruce isn't exactly doing or using any of this power I'm currently using on you. He is only acting as a conduit to this power."

John was shocked as well as in disbelief after Bruce or, to be accurate, Elizabeth had just told him. He couldn't believe Elizabeth was using Bruce's body as a conduit to her supernatural powers she has.

Chapter 14

Although John then realized that if she wanted to kill all of them and do it as fast as she wanted to, this power she was using on him would be capable of doing just that. A moment later, John felt as well as saw his left arm to being raised up and figured that it was Elizabeth's doing. When it was aligned to where his neck was, Bruce then said, "I hope you haven't forgotten what I told you I would be doing now."

After Bruce said that to John, he tried to remember exactly what he was telling him about. A short moment later, John was scared when he finally remembered what Bruce was asking him about. He remembered Elizabeth telling him that for cracking some bones in different places on Bruce's body he hit for the second time, she was going to crack one of his own.

John then said, "What exactly are you going to do with my left arm?"

Bruce replied with, "I know that you just remembered what I'm going to precisely do to your arm, just by the look you had on your face a moment ago."

John was both shocked and surprised to know Bruce had taken notice of that even though he wasn't that far away from him right now.

Bruce continued with, "If I'm needed to remind you then, so be it. I'm about to break your left arm in any way I want to hear the bones in it crack, just like you heard the bones in this body crack."

John was scared as well as wondered in what way was Elizabeth planning to break his arm. Then all of a sudden, John started to feel a strange tingling sensation go through his left arm, and that same feeling progressively got stronger as well as more painful. When he was no longer able to withstand the pain the moment the feeling in his left arm got to where it felt like it was in a fierce vise, John began to scream in agony as well as immeasurable suffering. A little while later, when John to sweat because of the pain and suffering he was currently going through, he asked, "What are you doing to me? Why do I feel like my entire left arm is in some kind of stinging vise?"

Bruce answered with, "Have you ever seen what happens when a full-grown boa constrictor gets a grip on any part of a person's body?"

John thought about it thoroughly for a moment, and when he finally realized what Bruce was asking him to see, John looked at his arm for a short moment and then at Bruce to ask, "You plan on breaking my arm the way a boa constrictor would do when it has a grip on a person's arm?"

Bruce nodded and said in response, "Yes, and that painful feeling you are currently experiencing in your left arm, well, imagine it to be a Boa creating a stronghold on your left arm that will end very soon badly for it as well as the person that is connected to it."

After Bruce said that, he smiled and laughed for a short moment. John tried to figure out what exactly Bruce was laughing and he meant with what he just told them. The moment John figured out everything he wanted to figure out, the pain started to get severe in the parts between the hand and elbow as well as the shoulder.

When he felt that happening to those parts of his arm, John immediately screamed in extreme pain and anguish. A moment later, John was starting to feel as if the bones in the parts of his left arm were being crushed by Elizabeth's supernatural force. After John noticed that, he then realized what Elizabeth wanted to do to him was going to happen very soon.

A moment later, John felt the bone between the hand and elbow break into two. Immediately following the tear of that bone, the one between the elbow and shoulder broke right away. In both times, John screamed loudly in extreme pain and tried to avoid becoming unconscious because of the amount of pain he was going through now.

John then said, "Well now, what are you going to do with me now that you have broken my arm?"

Bruce answered with, "I think I'm going to do just two more things to you, and that'll be it."

Then John asked, "And what exactly are those two last things you would like to do to me?"

Bruce said in response, "One is throwing you completely through the kitchen wall, and the second thing is to finally kill you."

The moment John heard that, he was wide awake as well as utterly frightened by the fact Elizabeth wanted to at last kill him, and knew she would go on to do the same to the others. When he realized what would occur the moment Elizabeth finished him off for good, John began to laugh as if Bruce told him a joke just now.

Then Bruce asked, "Why are you laughing? Did I say something funny to you?"

John looked at Bruce and said in response, "It isn't that. It's just that you should get on with what you want to do with me because I have been waiting for you to finish me off, believe it or not."

Bruce was baffled at what John just said and wondered if he was out of his mind because of the extreme amount of pain Elizabeth put him in when she broke his arm in pieces. Bruce then asked, "And exactly why is it that you want me to go ahead and kill you now?"

John answered with, "Because I thought I wouldn't have escaped from the reach this house has on us, and even if someone helped me walk or get out of this house as fast as possible, you would still be able to catch us as well as kill all of us, so I stayed behind to go before anyone else."

After John told Bruce as well as Elizabeth that, he seemed to be thinking if he should go on and kill him right away, like John said, or if he should continue on with what he said to him he was going to do next before really killing him. A moment later, Bruce said, "I think I have to deny your request for me to kill you right away because that wouldn't bring me no joy, so I'll go on with what I have already told you I was going to do to you next."

The moment he heard that, John made himself appear like he was completely disappointed with Bruce's answer to not kill him right away, but he was truly happy to know that. Then a short moment later, John started to feel something go throughout his body, and it reminded of the moment when Bruce pushed him toward the kitchen very hard.

When John realized that, he waited for the moment Bruce would it once again like before, but as far he had told him, he was going to make sure he went completely through the kitchen wall this time around. A short moment later, Bruce finally pushed John fiercely toward the kitchen wall. Then after John went completely through the wall and was now in the kitchen, Leslie wanted to go see if John was still alive, but Steve stopped her from doing so.

Leslie then asked, "What are you doing? Why aren't you not letting me go?"

Steve gave her a sign to quiet down as well as told her to stop talking. A moment later, when Leslie did what Steve told her to do, he pointed forward in the direction where they both saw John go through the kitchen wall all the way.

The moment Steve saw that Leslie had her sights in that direction, he whispered in her ear, "When you see Bruce, act as if you just came back inside and saw John through the kitchen wall when you did."

Leslie said in response, "And what will you do when you see Bruce yourself?"

Steve replied with, "I'm going to act like I'm wondering what could have pushed John so hard through the kitchen wall, but we already know that it was Elizabeth that did that to him, wouldn't you agree?"

Leslie thought about what Steve said to her for a moment, and found he was right. The person responsible of pushing John completely through the kitchen was Elizabeth while she was possessing Bruce's body. After she figured that out, Leslie said, "So what are we going to do if she does something else we can't allow? Because if you remember, Elizabeth is going to kill every single one of us without any amount of mercy when she finishes us off."

THE HAUNTED HOUSE

When he remembered that detail of what Elizabeth was going to do to them when she catches them, Steve said in response, "If either of us catches any signal that tell us that Elizabeth is going to finish John off first, we get something to use to get her away from him and then take him to the front door so we can light the wine streak, which you know what we need to do after that happens, right?"

Leslie immediately knew what Steve was leading her on to because after either of them lit the wine streak, they all needed to quickly get out of the house before it exploded by the gas some of them released from the kitchen's stove. After she realized that, Leslie nodded to tell Steve she understood, and waited for the moment to rescue John from Elizabeth's evil intentions.

A short while later, Bruce was finally in their sights, they knew what they needed to do next. Leslie and Steve started to act as well as show the expressions that wouldn't be found suspicious by Elizabeth's eyes. When Bruce looked at them, he made an evil smile that frightened Leslie inside and out while Steve wasn't frightened by it at all.

Bruce said loud enough to be heard by them, "Hey, you two, wait right there while I finish my business with your friend John." After Bruce said that, Leslie and Steve acted as if they were both worried and scared. When Bruce took his sight off them, Leslie looked around to find something she could use to make Bruce unable to go on with killing John in whatever way Elizabeth wanted to do it.

The moment Steve saw Bruce was inside the kitchen as well as finding something to use to ensure John's well-being from Elizabeth's wrath, he signaled for Leslie to quickly but silently go toward the kitchen. By the time they were halfway to the kitchen, Steve said, "Hey, Leslie, give me that wooden bat you found in the living room near the fireplace."

Leslie asked, "Why, what are you going to with it?"

Steve replied with, "I'm going to be the one that will hit Bruce with it while you are going to rescue John the moment I do that."

After he told Leslie that, she gave the wooden bat to Steve and followed with asking him where he was planning to hit Bruce with the bat.

Steve answered with, "Somewhere that would give you enough time to get John then quickly get out of the kitchen before he recovers from the hit."

Leslie thought about what place on Bruce's body would make it possible to do the things Steve wanted her to do after he hit him at that place on his body. When she figured out what part of Bruce's body Steve was going to hit with the bat she gave him, Leslie asked, "Are you going to hit Bruce in the head with the wooden bat?"

Steve said in response, "Yes I am. Can you think of another place on his body that would give you the time needed to rescue John and get out of the kitchen as fast as possible?"

When she realized Steve was right in hitting Bruce in the head, Leslie and he sped up to be there before Bruce killed John. A moment later, they were finally at the entrance to the kitchen. Steve and Leslie both found out they weren't too late in saving John from becoming the first of them to be killed by Elizabeth and doing it with the use if Bruce's body. After both of them found that they still have time to save John, Steve said, "Go to the entrance and distract Bruce so I can hit him without being noticed."

Leslie agreed with Steve's plan and quickly but silently went to the other entrance to the kitchen. The moment Leslie was at the other entrance, she waited for Steve to signal her to start distracting Bruce so he could hit him without being caught in his sights. When Steve gave her the sign to go ahead with distraction Bruce's attention on her, she immediately began to do whatever she came up with to get his sights kept on her, like loudly talking to him.

After Steve saw Bruce had his attention completely on Leslie, he silently walked up to him until he was directly behind him. The moment Steve was right behind Bruce, he started to set himself up to prepare to hit him in the head with the bat. When he was set to take the hit to Bruce's head, Steve took it when he found it good to do so.

When Steve hit Bruce in the head and knocked him out hard to the floor, Leslie quickly went to where John was at and tried to pick him up to his feet. By the time Leslie got John back on his feet, she put herself in his side because she noticed right away his left

THE HAUNTED HOUSE

arm was completely injured, and thought it was somehow caused by Elizabeth.

Once she was under John's right arm in case he had trouble walking the moment he went through the kitchen wall, Leslie told him to quickly follow her out of the kitchen and head toward the front door. Then after John was in sync with the speed Leslie was at to get quickly out of the kitchen and to the front door, Steve started following them while checking to see if Bruce had woken up or not, and inform the others of the moment he finally does get back on his feet.

The moment Leslie was almost back to where she and Steve were standing at around the time John was thrown viciously through the kitchen wall, she said, "Hey, Steve, is Bruce still out cold on the floor?"

Steve looked back to see if Bruce was but was starting to prepare himself, because he saw a shadow in the kitchen get up, which he immediately realized was Bruce's shadow getting up.

Chapter 15

After he realized Bruce was no longer out cold and was back on his feet, Steve replied with, "Get John outside, quick, and try to set yourself up at the end of the wine streak you made." Leslie knew if Steve was telling here to do those things, it meant Bruce was awake and probably going after them the moment he had them in his sights.

Then after knowing Bruce was now conscious again, John said, "Go to where you need to be at when Bruce gets out of the kitchen and comes after all of us."

Leslie asked, "And what are you going to do? Are you still able to walk on your own, especially in the condition you are currently in?"

John answered with, "Yeah, I'm still good to walk on my own, so go to where you need to be to light the streak and end this nightmare for everyone."

Leslie nodded in agreement with what John told her, and let him go to the front door and get out of the house while she went to where the streak she made. A moment later, Leslie was finally at the end of the wine streak and looked to see how far John was from the front door now. After she saw that he was barely getting outside the house, Leslie put her sights back to the direction of the kitchen to see if Bruce was out of there and was going for them the moment he did.

She saw Bruce was still in the kitchen for some reason but also saw Steve was standing in between the kitchen and where she was

THE HAUNTED HOUSE

standing. After she noticed that, Leslie asked, "What are you doing, Steve? Why are you standing there instead of coming to where I'm at?"

Steve said in response, "I'm going to keep Bruce occupied this time, but the moment he gets to what you feel is close to finishing me off at any time, light the streak no matter what."

After Steve told Leslie that, she thought it was good plan of action and agreed to do what he told her to go through in case things between him and Bruce get out of hand. A short while later, Bruce finally came out of the kitchen and had a demented smile on his face. Then Bruce said, "Were the two of you waiting for me to come out of the kitchen?"

Steve and Leslie both nodded. Bruce followed with, "Well, I apologize if I made you two wait too long, but I had to heal the injury this body sustained with the bat you have in your hands, Steve."

Then Steve asked, "How bad was the injury I gave Bruce's head that it would take so long to heal it?"

Bruce said in response, "Well, if I wasn't possessing your friend's body, he would have been killed by the hit you gave to his head." After Bruce told Steve and Leslie that, they both were scared by the fact the injury was that severe but were in a way happy Elizabeth had made sure Bruce didn't die from it.

When Steve and Leslie knew that, Bruce said, "I would have to think that with the looks on both of your faces you two are happy that I didn't let Bruce die from the injury, if I'm not mistaken."

Leslie replied with, "In a way, we are, because even though he isn't the one trying to kill us, it's still his body, and he will still probably suffer a minor amount of pain from the injury at some point since you are possessing him."

Steve followed with, "And we both know that you won't allow him to die since you want Bruce here in this house, where he will stay as your companion for the rest of his life."

Bruce smiled and then said, "Well, it would be a lie If I told the both of you that you're wrong, but I won't, because everything you two said is absolutely true about me never allowing Bruce to die, for he will be my personal companion for all eternity no matter if he wants to or not."

After Bruce said that to the others, Steve responded with, "If you do that to him, he will never be happy being your companion forever because he will try to figure out a way to escape your hold on him every time he is in this evil house of yours."

Bruce said in Elizabeth's voice, "I know he won't accept staying as my eternal companion, and he will try to find a way to get away from me, but I know of a way to make sure that never occurs."

Leslie then asked, "What way do you know that will guarantee that Bruce never escapes from you or this house ever?"

Bruce answered in Elizabeth's voice, "Both of you are looking at that way which will ensure me that Bruce never tries or comes up with any ideas to escape from being my eternal companion in my house."

The moment Steve and Leslie heard that, they were both horrified to know that every time Bruce tried to escape from Elizabeth and her evil house, she will possess him and do whatever she needs to do to make sure he doesn't try it again. Then a moment after they realized that, Steve said, "Well, if that is the case, I think Bruce would want me to do the one thing that would end this horrible experience he is going through right now."

Bruce asked, "And what would that one thing be?"

Steve leaped forward toward Bruce and said, "This is what he would want me to do." Steve tried to swing the bat once again to Bruce's head but was stopped by him when he grabbed it with his bare hand.

Bruce then said, "Let me guess, you're going to do the same thing you did in the kitchen, but this time with more than a single hit to his head, if I'm not mistaken?"

Steve didn't answer his question but was shocked Bruce figured that out right away.

Bruce followed with, "I'll take that silence as well as the expression on your face as a yes to what I said to you."

Bruce suddenly started to crush the bat until he finally broke it apart into two pieces. After Bruce broke the bat, Steve was holding the part of the bat where he had both his hands, while Bruce held the

THE HAUNTED HOUSE

part that was about to make contact to his head before he stopped it from causing serious damage the moment it did.

Then Bruce said, "Well, now that you no longer have a weapon to cause damage to this body, I think it's about time I respond in kind." Bruce immediately dropped the piece of the bat he had in his hand and reached for Steve's throat. When he got a hold of it, Bruce started to lift Steve off the floor and made a grip to his throat so he wouldn't choke him to death.

A moment later, Bruce said in Elizabeth's voice, "I think I should make you go through the same things I did to your friend John, but it should be different since we're in a different place then he and I were at the time." After he told Steve that, Bruce began to slam Steve brutally to the walls until it made serious damage to them.

After the walls on both sides had a gaping hole on them, Bruce asked, "Have you had enough, Steve? Or should I continue delivering pain to every part of your body?"

Steve laughed as the best he could with having on his throat and replied with, "If this is all you have planned to hurt me, then John was given some special treatment."

While he was telling Bruce that, Steve put his right hand behind his back and signaled Leslie to light the streak. After Leslie noticed that and figured out what he was trying to signal her to do, she quickly got out a matchstick and lit it. Leslie then dropped the match on the streak, and it immediately caught on fire.

Once the streak caught on fire, it spread rapidly from where Leslie dropped the match to where she started the wine streak. The moment the burning streak was about to go by Steve and Bruce, Bruce took his attention off Steve while he was slamming him to another part of the left wall. When he had his sights on the streak that was on fire go passed by both of them, Bruce was about to return his attention back on Steve before he felt a hard hit to the back of his head and made him land hard to the floor face first. After Bruce got hit to behind his head, he immediately released his hold on Steve's throat.

The moment Steve was free from Bruce's hold on his throat, he ran toward Leslie while trying to catching to his breath as well as massaging his throat. The moment he was about to get to where Leslie was, Steve said, "Run, Leslie, head to the door before it's too late to get out of this house."

Leslie teared up for a moment but nodded. After she started to run toward the front door, Leslie and Steve were heading to it side by side, and both started to speed up so both of them got out of the house before the fire got to the kitchen. A moment later, Steve and Leslie finally got to the door. When Steve got to the door open, both of them looked behind for a short moment of time to see the progress of the burning streak and find out if Bruce was back on his feet again.

Steve and Leslie saw Bruce was barely getting in his feet while the fire was about to get to the kitchen in a short moment. After Leslie and Steve discovered that, they went outside and closed the door behind them. When both of them were outside of the house, they ran away to get some distance before the explosion occurred.

A moment later, the explosion Leslie and Steve were waiting for finally happened. It was more loud as well as destructive than they expected to come from the gas leak. Leslie fell to the ground from the explosion while Steve tripped but stayed up on his feet. After the explosion destroyed every part of the house, Steve was standing up and watching that happened as Leslie was still on the ground, looking away from the house.

When Steve noticed Leslie was keeping her sights away from the house, he asked, "Why are you keeping your sights off the house?."

Leslie looks at Steve and replied with, "I don't want to look at the destroyed house because then I will think of Bruce burning alive or anything else that would happen to him in the explosion."

Steve then realized Leslie had a good reason to not look at the house, for she was in love with Bruce. A short while later, the house was finally destroyed at every part, and the only things that seemed to be still standing were the posts or pillars that were the parts to keep the house up for a long time as the owners wanted to keep the place up.

Steve told Leslie the house was demolished at every part. After Leslie was standing up beside Steve, she found out that he was telling her the truth, which made her happy and sad, but mostly sad of knowing that. Steve looked at Leslie to see she had an expression on her face that didn't surprise him when he noticed it.

Steve knew Leslie was happy that the house was destroyed like they all wanted but was sad because it came with the cost of the man she confessed her love for before he got possessed by an evil ghost that haunted the house. When he saw Leslie start to cry all of a sudden, Steve said, "I know that you have mixed emotions about the destruction of the house since it came with the cost of Bruce's life, but you should know that he wasn't himself the moments before the explosion but Elizabeth, who was trying to kill all of us with his body."

Leslie nodded in agreement with what Steve was telling her. Steve then continued with, "And you know that Bruce told all of us to go through with destroying the house no matter what happens to him the moment it finally happened, because he wanted to die instead of being trapped forever in this house with that evil woman."

Then from out of nowhere, Steve and Leslie started to hear a sound from where they thought was the center of the demolished house. The sound both of them were hearing was the sound of something crumbling. After they found out where the sound was coming from, both of them saw that something was getting up from the ground.

A moment later, whatever was coming up from the ground was standing, and the others tried to focus on finding out what it was that came up from the ground. When Steve and Leslie found out what it was, they were both shocked and surprised to discover that it was Bruce who came up from the ground. They saw that Bruce had a lot of cuts on his body as well as severe burns on the left side of his face and arm.

Chapter 16

A short while later, Bruce looked up to see the others and was angry the moment he saw them. After he saw them, Bruce started to walk toward Steve and Leslie but was staggering while doing so. Bruce also seemed to be healing his injuries and burns progressively. With every step Bruce took to get closer to the others, Steve and Leslie stepped back to get a bit more distance from him.

By the time he got to where the entrance of the house would be at if the entire place had still been standing, Bruce had healed all his cuts and burns that he had on him. Bruce began to clean the dirt off his face that was left from the burn he had completely healed. The moment Bruce got all the dirt off his face, he looked behind him, and was looking at every direction like he was searching for something.

After he stopped looking behind him, Bruce got his sights back on Steve and Leslie. When he did, Bruce seemed to the others to have a furious expression on his face, which frightened Leslie just by looking at it.

Bruce then said in Elizabeth's voice, "How dare you do this! Look at what you have done to my beloved house." He continued to scream and or rant at Steve and Leslie about the destruction of her house for a short moment, and did so in Elizabeth's voice as well.

When Bruce finished shouting at the others, he appeared to be waiting for Steve and Leslie to reply. When they didn't respond to what Bruce told them, a voice said, "That was always the plan since the moment things began to get both weird and crazy as well as dangerous for everyone."

Steve and Leslie looked behind them to see who said that. They found out that it was John who said those things.

John continued with, "Did you ever wonder why we were burning every part of you house, or did you think we were just doing that to be destructive?"

Bruce replied with, "I didn't expect all of you to destroy my house completely. How did you do that?"

John answered with, "We came up with a plan at the last moment to destroy it with an explosive that would be big enough to do it, which wasn't that difficult to find something that can create it."

Bruce asked John what it was that made the explosion that completely destroyed Elizabeth's house until it was nothing but rubble. Then John said in response, "We used something in the kitchen that would give us the fuel to create an explosion. Can you guess what it was exactly?."

Bruce thought about it. A moment later, he said, "All of you used the gas from the stove to create the explosion. But how did you get it to explode?"

John laughed for a short moment and followed with, "As if you don't know. Or did the explosion also affect your memory?"

Bruce tried to remember what exactly created the explosion other than the gas from the stove in the kitchen. The moment he realized what made the explosion with the kitchen stove's gas, Bruce said, "That burning streak I saw before I was hit from the back of my head by something while I had Steve in my grasp."

After Bruce told the others that, Steve replied with, "It was not something random that hit you behind the head. I kicked you hard in the back of your head for good reasons."

Bruce then asked, "And what exactly are those reasons?"

Steve answered with, "One is to get free from your hold, and the second is to get out of the house before the explosion happened."

Then after Steve told Bruce the reasons for kicking him behind the head, he appeared to the others to have gotten even more furious as well as angry than before. After John and the others noticed that, they all knew why. A moment later, Bruce said, "So you kicked me from behind the head to get out of the way when the burning streak got to the kitchen and then exploded?"

Steve nodded to answer Bruce's question. Bruce then said in Elizabeth's voice, "If that's the case, then I should personally kill all of you here and do the same to the rest that are in the vehicle over there by the gates."

After Elizabeth said that to the others, they began to witness something strange occur to Bruce. Bruce seemed to be going through some kind of spasm that went through his entire body. It worried the others just by seeing that happen to him. A moment later, Bruce quickly went down on his knees and put his hands down the moment he was on the ground.

When Bruce was on the ground on his knees with his head down, John and the others wondered why Bruce was having some type of full-body spasm. A moment later, Leslie started to walk toward Bruce but didn't get far because Steve stopped her from going any closer to him. Leslie then asked, "Why did you stop me from seeing if Bruce is back to his normal self?"

Steve told her to allow him to do that so that she doesn't get hurt or worse if it turns out that Bruce wasn't back. Leslie thought about what Steve told her for a moment and then nodded to tell him to go ahead with finding out if Bruce is back with them or not. When Steve was about to touch Bruce on the shoulder, he saw that he flinched for an instant.

After he saw that, Steve stepped a few steps back and waited for something else to happen. A moment later, Bruce quickly got back to his feet and started to crack a few bones from his arms to end at his neck. After Bruce ended the bone cracking at his neck, he lifted his head slowly until it was in the direction of looking at the others when he opened his eyes.

The moment he had his head in that direction, Bruce opened his eyes, and the others were shocked and surprised by his eyes. Bruce's eyes appeared to be white to the others. This was why they were surprised and shocked the moment he opened them. Then all of a sudden, Bruce began to scream, and it was a strange one at that.

THE HAUNTED HOUSE

John and the others noticed the scream was combining Bruce's and Elizabeth's voices together for some reason. A short time later, Elizabeth came out of Bruce's body and flew toward Steve. The moment Elizabeth left Bruce's body, he fell backward to the ground. When Elizabeth got a hold of Steve's throat and started to lift him off the ground, Bruce landed hard on his back on the ground as well.

A moment later, Elizabeth was about a few feet above the ground with Steve in one of hands. Leslie then said, "What are you doing, Elizabeth? Why do you have Steve up off the ground and holding his throat with your hand?"

Elizabeth looked at Leslie and replied with, "I already told you what I'm going to do, or did you not listen?"

Leslie tried to remember what it was Elizabeth had told them about what she was going to do next. When Leslie finally remembered what Elizabeth was going to do next, she got scared and was frightened by it as well.

Elizabeth sighed and said, "By the look on your face, it seems that you have at last remembered what I'm going to do next."

Leslie said in response, "You are going to finish everyone off here and then go after the others to do the same to them."

Elizabeth followed with, "And I'm going to start with your friend Steve first and continue from there." After she told the others that, she began to stretch her left arm behind her back. When Leslie and John saw that, both of them realized she was about to attack Steve in any way Elizabeth wanted to with her left arm.

The moment Elizabeth had her arm set to attack Steve, she looked at the others and said, "I hope you watch closely as I kill your friend here."

Leslie saw Elizabeth had made her hand into what seemed like a spear, which she knew that meant she was going to stab Steve with. Before Elizabeth's hand was about to hit Steve at the stomach, Leslie screamed at Elizabeth to stop and to not go through with the attack on him.

When Elizabeth's hit finally landed on Steve's stomach, something strange occurred immediately when it did. Leslie and John witnessed as most of Elizabeth's left arm crumble into rubble. After that happened, Elizabeth's other arm started to do the same, which freed Steve from her grasp. After Steve was free from Elizabeth's hold, he fell to the ground and landed roughly.

Steve coughed and tried to catch his breath as well as massage his throat from the soreness he began to feel from it. The moment Steve felt okay from his throat, he got up to his feet and walked back to the others. After Steve was with Leslie and John, they all put their attention back to Elizabeth and watched as strange things continued to happen to her.

Elizabeth looked at what was left of both of her arms and saw the veins in them start to burn as well as light up. The burns in her veins quickly spread throughout her body, and Elizabeth seemed to be getting scared by it. While that was happening, Elizabeth slowly descended to the ground. A moment later, Elizabeth finally got back to the ground and the spread of whatever was going through her body.

After that was completed, Elizabeth looked at the others and began to get angry the moment she had them in her sights. "This is all your fault, because whatever is happening to me, it has something to do with you people destroying my precious house."

John replied with, "Even if that were the case, I think that none of us are regretting doing it."

When Leslie and Steve nodded in agreement with what John said, Elizabeth appeared to have gotten more enraged than before. Elizabeth was about to leap toward them before both of her legs seemed to be changing color for some reason. Elizabeth's legs were changing from their usual color to charcoal, and were doing so progressively.

A moment later, both of Elizabeth's legs had completely turned to charcoal. When Elizabeth tried to move one of her legs, it suddenly crumbled the same way her arms did. Elizabeth tried to keep her balance with the one leg she still had, but it crumbled as well in a short amount of time. After both of her legs were gone and had turned to rubble, Elizabeth was on the ground with what was left of the half of her body.

Elizabeth seemed sad by the fact she longer had her legs, but something else immediately started to occur. Whatever was happening to her legs began to occur throughout the rest of her body, starting from the bottom and slowly going to the top. When Elizabeth saw that happen, she repeatedly yelled no and didn't accept whatever was occurring to her now.

Then a moment later, whatever was spreading slowly to her head was only halfway there, and Elizabeth appeared to be getting tired of both yelling as well not accepting what was happening to her. After she stopped yelling, Elizabeth looked at the others with an angry expression, as if she was to explode on them with her fury in some way.

Elizabeth started to shout at the others for everything that had happened, including what was occurring to her right now. The moment whatever was going through her got to her head, Elizabeth appeared to be freezing up in the movement of her face as well as every part of her body, including her head. When she was completely frozen in place, Elizabeth had the look of her still screaming at them and utter anger toward them too.

A moment later, Elizabeth suddenly began to crumble, and the others watched closely as it was happening. After she was nothing but rubble, Leslie and the others walked to the rubble. When they got to where the rubble of Elizabeth's body was, all of them looked at what remained of Elizabeth's body, which was nothing but rubble. They also saw it had progressively turned to dust.

After all of them saw that, Leslie led the others to where Bruce was at lying flat on the ground. The moment everyone was standing around Bruce's down body, Leslie checked to see if he was still alive after Elizabeth left his body. Leslie said, "Bruce, are you still with us?"

After Leslie said that but didn't get a response from Bruce, she looked to see if he had a pulse or not. By the time Leslie found the best spot on Bruce's body to find a pulse, which was on his neck, she checked to find out if he still had a pulse. A moment later, Leslie took her hand off, and the others saw that she had a depressed look on her face.

Steve then asked, "What's wrong, Leslie? Why do you have such a sad as well as depressed look on your face?."

John followed with, "Did you find a pulse on Bruce's neck?"

Leslie shook her head and replied with, "No, I didn't find or feel a pulse at all, which means Bruce is actually…"

Chapter 17

The others immediately realized what it meant, and they all began to feel very sad by that realization. After they started to feel that way by the discovery of Bruce's death, all of them now knew why Leslie had a depressed look on her face the moment she couldn't find a pulse on him. A moment later, Leslie began to cry as well as put her head on Bruce's chest. While Leslie was doing that, the others let her get her feelings out because they knew what she felt about him.

A short while later, Leslie stopped crying and started to clear her face from the tears. After she finished clearing her face of her shed tears, Leslie stood up and asked, "What do you guys want to do with Bruce's body? I don't want to leave him here."

The others thought about it thoroughly for a moment and then agreed to take Bruce's body with them instead of leaving him where they were at still.

Leslie then said, "Thank you for agreeing to take Bruce's body with us and not leaving him at this evil place."

John responded with, "I think the one thing that mostly helped us with the decision was putting both your opinion as well as your feelings for Bruce."

Leslie thanked them once more, and wanted to know how they were going to take Bruce's body into the shuttle bus.

Steve then said, "I have a blanket inside my luggage. We could put Bruce's body in the middle of it and carry him all the way to the shuttle."

The others thought Steve's idea could work. Leslie followed with, "I think that is a good plan. Let's do it."

Everyone agreed to do Steve's plan to move Bruce's body to the shuttle bus. All began to head toward the shuttle to get the blanket out of Steve's luggage bag as well as figure out where they were going to put his body in the shuttle without giving up anyone's luggage.

After the first few steps to the shuttle, everyone heard the sound of someone taking a deep breath behind all of them. The moment all of them heard that from behind them, they immediately realized there could only be one thing that would be making the sound they heard. Leslie quickly turned her sights behind her to see if what she and the others realized what could have made the sound they all heard.

When she saw Bruce was breathing again, Leslie went to where he was left as fast as she could. The moment Leslie finally got to where Bruce was, she said, "Are you with us, Bruce?"

Leslie repeated saying that a couple of times until Bruce responded with, "I'm with you."

After Bruce replied to Leslie's calls to him to see if he was with them, Leslie shouted, telling the others Bruce was alive now and for them to come over to see for themselves.

A moment later, the others were finally at where Leslie was and saw Bruce really was alive again, which made them relieved and happy to know that but mostly happy. The moment everyone else saw Bruce was no longer dead but alive, John asked, "Hey, Bruce, how are you feeling right now?"

Bruce responded with, "Well, to tell you the truth, right now I feel I just got dog piled by a football team."

After he told everyone how he was feeling at the moment, Steve then asked, "Are you still able to walk, or at least stand?"

Bruce then said, "I don't know, but let's find out if I still can." He tried to get up with his arms but fell to the ground in pain.

THE HAUNTED HOUSE

After the first few tries that ended with him falling to the ground in pain, Bruce gave up and asked for someone to help him to get up on his feet to find out if he can still walk or stand. Steve answered Bruce's call for help, and began to get him up to his feet to see if he can still stand or walk by himself. A moment later, Steve finally got Bruce up to his feet and asked, "Are you ready to see if you can still move on your own?"

Bruce nodded. When Steve let go of Bruce, he right away started to move forward but fell to the ground on the first step. Bruce was in utter pain the moment he landed hard on the ground to his left side. Everyone went to where Bruce fell, and Leslie then asked, "Are you all right, Bruce? What happened?"

Bruce answered with, "I don't know exactly, but I think both of my legs just went completely numb for some reason." After Bruce told the others that, John said in response, "Well, if that is the case, I think that me and someone else should carry you all the way to the shuttle bus."

Bruce then asked, "How are you going to carry me? That needs two people."

John replied with, "You are going to put your arms around mine and the other person's shoulder so the both of us can move you to the shuttle bus while at the same time try to get rid of the numbness in both of your legs."

After John told Bruce that, he said, "I think that is a great idea, but who will help you do that?"

Steve responded with, "I will, if John would like me to help him with his idea to get Bruce to the shuttle bus."

John answered with, "Sure, Steve, you can help me out. Which side do you want to cover?"

The moment Steve picked the left side, John immediately went to the right side and said, "We will start moving when you're ready."

A moment later, Steve said, "Ready to go."

John nodded, and both started to move in unison toward the shuttle bus. While they were moving to the shuttle, John asked Bruce to try moving his legs to get rid of the numbness faster. After he agreed to do so, Bruce started to move his legs the best he could but wasn't able to stay standing with every single step they took toward the shuttle bus.

A short while later, Bruce began to get some feelings back into his legs. It made him very happy to feel that happening. By the time he had all feelings back in his legs, and told the others that, Steve then asked, "Do you want to see if you are now able to move on your own?"

Bruce responded with, "Yes, let's see if I can move to the shuttle bus on my own."

The moment John and Steve let go of Bruce, they saw he was able to stand on his own, and quickly started to move toward the shuttle bus. When the others saw Bruce was able to move without any problems, they also began to go to the shuttle bus as well. A while later, Bruce was the first one to get to the shuttle bus, and waited for the others so they could all go wherever all of them decided to go to.

By the time the others finally got the shuttle, Lora opened the middle door and greeted them for their return as well as completely destroying the entire house to the ground. John replied with, "Well, we did face some problems in the way before doing just that."

Steve followed with, "But it was mostly one problem that was holding us back from destroying the whole house."

Lora then asked, "What was the problem that was stopping you from destroying the house?"

The others hesitated to tell her, but Bruce said, "It was Elizabeth. She was the one that was stopping us from destroying the house and did everything she could to not let that happen."

Lora replied with, "What exactly did Elizabeth do to stop all of you from finishing what everyone agreed to do after finding out that the house was haunted by her, and was probably going after all of us so she could do the same thing she did to Earl?"

Bruce said in response, "Well, I don't know if Marissa, you, or Ben know this. But the first thing that Elizabeth wanted to do was to take complete control as well as possession over my body."

After the others saw a surprised look on Lora's face, Steve asked, "By the way, Lora, how is Ben doing?"

Lora told everyone that seemed all right but still needed professional help with his injuries. She then asked the others if what Bruce said was true.

After everyone nodded, John said, "And if you tried hit him while he was being possessed, it wouldn't do any permanent physical damage to him at all."

Lora then asked, "Why would anyone confront Bruce if you and the others knew that he was possessed?"

John replied with, "It was to allow the others to do a plan I came up with before they got back to the first floor."

Marissa then asked, "What was your plan about?"

John said in response, "To completely demolish the house by making an explosion with the gas from the stove in the kitchen and making a streak with wine from in the kitchen to halfway to the front door, which one of us would light once we were all far away from the kitchen."

Leslie followed with, "I was the one who got to do that and lit it when the time was right."

After Leslie said that, Lora asked, "What exactly do you mean that you lit the streak of wine the moment it was right to do so?"

Leslie answered with, "We had to wait for Elizabeth, or should I say Bruce, to be near the kitchen when it explodes and make sure that John wasn't killed or left anywhere near there when it happened."

Lora and Marissa looked at John more closely and immediately noticed he was battered all over, but mostly in his left arm. Marissa then asked, "What happened to your left arm, John?"

John said in response, "Elizabeth made Bruce break it like a boa constrictor."

Lora followed with, "How is that possible?"

John answered with, "I don't exactly know how it happened either, but all I felt at the time was a strong sensation go throughout my left arm that turned into a painful sensation and ended with breaking majority of my left arm."

After John told Lora and Marissa that, he said, "Then I was thrown through the kitchen wall without mercy."

Then Lora asked, "And what were you two doing when that happened?"

Steve answered with, "You two might think that we were standing still from where we were at while that was happening, but I had an idea that I would rescue John from any further harm and buy us time to get him away."

Marissa replied with, "How exactly did you two buy time to get John away from Elizabeth's clutches?"

Leslie said in response, "I distracted Bruce so that Steve would be able to sneak attack him and hit Bruce in the head with a wooden bat."

Lora then asked, "And did hitting Bruce in the head buy the time both of you needed to get John away from there?"

Steve nodded. "Yes, it did, and when John was outside, I had Leslie to go back to the end of the streak of wine so she could light it whenever she wanted to do it."

Lora followed with, "And what were you going to be doing?"

Steve then said, "I was going to get Bruce's attention and keep it so he doesn't stop Leslie from lighting the streak the moment he notices Leslie as well as the streak near her."

Chapter 18

After Steve told the others that, Marissa said, "How did you keep Bruce's attention only on you?"

Steve answered with, "Well, it might have been crazy in doing what I did to have his attention only on me, but I got his full attention by attacking him with the bat I had at the moment."

Lora said in response, "That is crazy. You knew that Bruce couldn't take any permanent damage at the time."

Steve nodded and said, "Even though I did know that, it was the only way to draw his attention towards me."

Marissa then asked, "And what happened when you had Bruce's attention kept on just you?"

Steve said in response, "Well, it went good at the start but progressively got worse for me."

Lora replied with, "How exactly did it get worse for you?"

Steve then said, "Bruce quickly reacted when I tried to hit him once more to his head, and it was after that things got worse."

Lora followed with, "What did Bruce do after he reacted to the second strike to his head?"

Steve answered with, "Bruce broke the bat and then grabbed me by the throat that he followed with him slamming me against the walls of the hallway until they were seriously damaged." Steve continued on with telling the others that after the walls were both damaged, he signaled Leslie the best way he could at the moment to light the streak because he thought Bruce was going to finish him off.

After Steve told the others that, Leslie said, "After I noticed that he was signaling me, I lit a match and dropped it on the streak."

Steve followed with, "And Bruce took his attention off me to the burning streak the moment it was about to go by us, which gave me the chance to free myself from his hold."

After Marissa asked him how he freed himself from Bruce's grasp, Steve answered with, "By hitting him behind the head with a kick I put as much strength I could make at the moment, and it ended up being enough to get me free."

Lora then asked, "What did you do after you were finally free?"

Steve said in response, "I caught my breath for a moment and then ran towards Leslie as fast as I could."

Leslie continued with, "When Steve was about to get to where I was, he told me to run towards the front door before the fire got to the kitchen." By the time they got to the part of the story where the two of them were finally at the front door of the house, Steve said, "Both of us looked behind to check how far the fire was from the kitchen as well as to see if Bruce was back on his feet too."

Marissa then asked, "What did the both of you find out?"

Steve answered with, "The fire was about to get to the kitchen."

Leslie followed with, "And Bruce was barely getting back on his feet." After Leslie said that, Lora said, "Did you get out of the house after seeing that?"

They both nodded. After both of them told Lora what she wanted to know, Steve said, "When we were outside, both of us quickly started to run as far away from the house as we could to avoid the blast from the explosion."

Leslie followed with, "And the moment the explosion finally happened, you can see how much damage it did to the whole house."

Marissa and Lora both looked at the house and saw what the extent was of the explosion the others were telling them about. They saw the damage the explosion had to the house was very severe, which made them both happy since that was what they wanted to

THE HAUNTED HOUSE

happen to the entire house, even though it wasn't by the way all of them wanted or had planned to do so.

A moment later, Ben said, "Is everyone here already?"

Lora replied with, "Yes, everyone is finally here, and the house is completely destroyed as well."

Ben slowly got himself up to see if Lora was telling him the truth about the house being destroyed. A short while later, Ben asked, "How was the house destroyed? I can see it wasn't by the fire, like we had all planned."

Steve said in response, "You are right, the house wasn't destroyed by fire, but instead it was an explosion John, Leslie, and I made at the last moment."

Ben replied with, "What did you all use to make an explosion that would have enough destructive power to demolish the entire house?"

Leslie told Ben everything she and the others have already informed Marissa and Lora about how the house was destroyed completely.

A short while later, after Leslie finished telling Ben everything about the destruction of the entire house, he asked them what they were going to do next, because he wanted to get proper treatment for his injuries and if anyone else who got hurt wanted to do the same.

John then said, "I think that is a great idea to get everyone that got hurt treated properly, and to do so, I think we should head back home."

The others thought about what John said to them and agreed it was a great idea since most of them did have injuries that needed proper medical treatment. After everyone agreed to go back home to get those who are injured treated, Ben asked, "Who is going to drive the shuttle bus all the way home?"

Before anyone could respond, they all began to hear a wailing sound. Everyone immediately noticed that it was the same sound they heard when Earl's ghost appeared to them. After everyone recognized the wailing sound, they turned around to see if it was Earl's ghost that was making it. The moment all of them saw Earl's ghost, they were happy to see he no longer seemed to be suffering, but the wailing sound still went on.

Steve then asked, "Why is the wailing sound still going on even though Earl's spirit is right in front of us?"

Earl answered with, "That is because I wasn't the only spirit that was trapped in that house by Elizabeth's will."

Lora followed with, "Who else was trapped in the house with you?"

Earl said in response, "Some of Elizabeth's husbands as well as a few maids and other people, but if all of you don't believe me, just wait and see for yourselves."

A moment later, more spirits started to take form before all of them, and they recognized some of them. Earl was telling them the truth when he told everyone that some of Elizabeth's husbands were also trapped with him. Another thing, everyone saw other than the maids there were also a couple of people who appeared to be gardeners, by the clothes they were wearing. After all the other spirits appeared and the wailing sound ended the moment the last spirit appeared, Leslie then asked, "What is going to happen to all of you since the house is destroyed?"

After all the spirits, including Earl, smiled when Leslie asked them that question, he answered with, "We are all going to pass on to the next life and find peace."

When each of the spirits began to disappear, they all thanked the group for releasing them from the torment all of them were going through at the hands of Elizabeth.

A moment later, Earl was the only spirit still standing before the others. Then Steve asked, "What is wrong? Why have you not passed on like the other spirits that were trapped in the house?"

Earl replied with, "Because I want to make sure you all know of something in case everyone didn't notice."

John followed with, "And what would that be?"

Earl said in response, "Well, that James Griffin wasn't among the spirits that appeared before all of you."

When Earl told the others that, everyone tried to remember all the spirits that belonged to the husbands Elizabeth murdered for their belongings. A short while later, the others realized Earl was right, the spirit of James Griffin wasn't among the other late husbands. Bruce then asked, "Why is James's spirit not with the others since he was also murdered by Elizabeth as well as the first one to be killed?"

Earl answered with, "Even though he was killed by Elizabeth, like the other husbands, James was the one that made her into a killer."

When the group heard that, all of them realized what it meant. They knew the exact reason why James's spirit was among those that were trapped in the house after they were all killed by Elizabeth.

After everyone realized why James wasn't trapped like the others, Earl's spirit started to progressively disappear. Before he completely disappeared, Earl said, "Thanks, everyone, for what you all have done to free the others and me from the torment by Elizabeth's hand." After Earl disappeared from their sights, everyone was happy to know they had helped Earl as well as others from their entrapment in the house by the evil powers Elizabeth somehow gotten over time, possibly by the people she killed for her selfish reasons.

A moment later, everyone got into the shuttle bus but avoided sitting on the corner left side of the vehicle that had the smaller tire compared to the others. After that, they were all in the places that all of them found to be necessary so they could go back on the road to their town. Then Bruce said, "I think we should go to the gas station we passed on the way here and see if it's open this time."

The others thought about what Bruce told them for a short moment to see if they wanted to go and do that. Everyone agreed to go and see if the gas station was open so they can get the tire they needed to get back home in comfort, in case all of them were going back in places they were currently sitting in and felt uncomfortable for them.

A while later, the group were about to get close to the gas station, and they could all see that it was open by the lights that were going through the entire place. After everyone saw that, Bruce asked, "What do you guys think we should also get from the gas station?"

Steve answered with, "Probably some of the items to treat the injuries most of us have, especially Ben, and maybe some snacks for the entire way back."

Everyone thought Steve was right in getting all of the things he thought they should get from the gas station for the road back home. When they finally got to the gas station, Bruce stopped in the center of the station and said, "Everyone, go get what we agreed to buy from the gas station while I get the tire we need to even out the shuttle bus."

After everyone got out of the shuttle bus and walked to the gas station, Bruce parked in front of the garage to an auto shop. The moment he was in front of the garage to the auto shop, Bruce saw a sign that said to honk to get service, and right away did just that. A moment later, the garage door started to go up progressively.

Chapter 19

By the time the garage door was completely up and open, he saw a man was standing in the entryway. When the man was at the driver's window where Bruce was, he asked, "My name is Mike, and what do you need help with?"

Bruce answered with, "I need to replace a tire that is a different size compared to the others."

Mike replied with, "Do you know what tire is the one that is different?"

Bruce told Mike it was the last tire in the back on his side of the shuttle bus. After Bruce told him that, Mike went to check the tire to find out the size difference to the other tires. A short while later, Mike finished changing the tire and went to the driver's window again. When he got to the window, Mike asked, "How would you like to pay for the tire?"

Bruce then asked, "Can I pay with card?"

Mike nodded. After Mike charged the card Bruce gave him, he said, "Would you like to have the receipt, or would you like me to tear it up?"

Bruce replied with, "You can give me the receipt, if you would like." Then after Mike gave him the receipt, Bruce thanked Mike for the service and went to the front of the gas station.

The moment Bruce was parked in front of the gas station, everyone had the stuff they went inside to get, except Ben. When Bruce noticed that, he asked, "Why are you not carrying anything, Ben?"

Ben said in response, "Because I started to feel in serious pain again as well as have bleeding in some of the cuts."

After Ben told Bruce that, he looked to see of he was really bleeding in the cuts he had. When he saw Ben was indeed bleeding in some of his cuts, Bruce asked for whoever had the bag with the medical items to treat Ben as soon as they can. Even though John was the one who had the bag with the medical items, he didn't know how to treat Ben's cut so they would stop bleeding for until all of them got back home.

When Lora volunteered to treat Ben's opened cuts, John gave her the items needed to do just that in one of her bags. A moment later, everyone got into the shuttle bus except Ben and Lora. Lora told Ben to sit down on the floor that was in the opening of the center door.

Ben then said, "I think that it would be better if I stand while you treat my opened cuts."

Lora asked, "Why do you think that would be better?"

Ben answered with, "Because I think the cuts would get more worse than they already are, and maybe even more cuts will start to open as well." After he told Lora that, she thought Ben might be right of what could occur if Ben sat down to get treated.

Then after she realized that having Ben sit down to treat his opened cuts might have consequences to his current condition, Lora let him stand to get his cuts treated. Ben took off his shirt so that it didn't get in the way of Lora treating his opened cuts. A short while later, Lora finished treating all of Ben's opened cuts, and she saw he had an expression of no longer being in any kind of pain on his face but that of relief and content.

A moment later, Ben put his shirt back on carefully and then got inside the shuttle bus first before Lora. After they got in the shuttle bus and were both seated, Bruce asked them if they were all right and ready to go. When Ben and Lora both told him that they were both okay and ready to go, Bruce turned on the shuttle bus started to drive back on the road home.

A while later, everyone saw they were halfway to getting home. This made them happy. By the time they got home, Bruce asked, "Should I stop at the hospital to drop off Ben so he could get his injuries treated, or should I go to our street so everyone can get off and then I can go to the hospital with Ben?"

Ben responded with, "You can drop me off at the hospital so you can take everyone home to relax."

Steve then said, "What about the shuttle bus, should you return it today or tomorrow?"

Ben answered with, "I think Bruce should return it tomorrow since it's late already."

After Ben told the others that, they thought he might have a point of it being really late to return the shuttle bus.

A moment later, Bruce stopped at the entrance of the hospital so Ben could get immediate treatment for all his wounds and injuries that were causing him a lot of pain. When Ben got off the shuttle bus, Lora followed him to the hospital. No one said anything about it. After Ben and Lora were in the hospital, Bruce drove the shuttle bus to the street all of them lived on.

When Bruce got to their street, he parked the shuttle bus on the street in front of his house. Everyone got off the shuttle bus and went to the trunk to get all their luggage out. After they got out all their luggage from the trunk, everyone went to their homes to put their luggage all of them had taken on the trip.

The moment all of them left their luggage inside their houses, they met back at the shuttle bus. After they were all back at the shuttle bus, Sarah asked, "What do you guys think we should do now? I want to go check up on Ben at the hospital to see how he is doing, and I probably won't be able to sleep after all of the things we went through at that demented house."

Bruce replied with, "I think Lora will call one of us to let us know how Ben is doing after getting his injuries treated, and we have to try to sleep even after the events we went through in that house."

The moment the others agreed to try to sleep in their houses and not worry about Ben's well-being because any of them would get a call from Lora or maybe himself, they all headed to their homes to try to relax and hopefully go to sleep without any problems in doing so.

When Bruce got into his house, he went to his room and started to take his clothes off so he could take a shower before trying to go to sleep. A short while later, Bruce finished taking a shower and dried off in the bathroom. While he was drying off, Bruce looked at himself in the window and started to feel strange for some reason.

Bruce began to have flashes of everything that had happened before and after Elizabeth possessed his body to kill all his friends. Bruce noticed the flashes end at the moment of the explosion from the kitchen that ended up destroying the entire house. When the flashes stopped completely, Bruce splashed water to his face to wake himself up and know that the nightmare is over and Elizabeth is gone for good.

A moment later, Bruce put on underwear and then went to bed. Bruce was having trouble going to sleep, so he tried to position himself in a way that would be comfortable enough to put him to sleep. By the time he finally found a position that felt really comfortable, Bruce slowly went to sleep, which he was happy to know.

A short while later, inside Bruce's dream, he was in his home fully clothed and was hearing a strange noise go throughout the house. He tried to focus on where exactly the strange noise was coming from. The moment he found out that it was coming from the front door, Bruce began to slowly go to the door so he could find out who or what was making the strange noise.

When he finally got to the door, Bruce suddenly started to hear his name and noticed the voice that was saying his name sounded familiar to him. A moment later, Bruce was frightened when he figured out who was saying his name in the voice from the front door of his house. After he figured that out, Bruce stepped back and said, "It can't be. We thought that with destroying the house you would be gone forever from our lives."

THE HAUNTED HOUSE

The voice laughed for a moment and replied with, "Well then, would it not mean that you didn't destroy the house completely?"

Suddenly, hard knocks began to hit the door. The knocks were causing a lot of damage to it. By the time the door seemed to about to give out, Bruce was near the wall that was close to his room as well as in complete fear of finding out the person who was saying his name was someone he and the others thought was gone from their lives for good.

Then after the front door finally gave out, it somehow got sucked outside and left the front doorway entrance wide open. When Bruce saw a figure in the pitch-black darkness of the outside, he recognized the figure and shook his head in utter disbelief. A moment later, the dark figure came inside Bruce's house and turned out to be Elizabeth in her ordinary form.

After she was in his house, Elizabeth said, "Hello, Bruce, are you shocked to see me?"

Although he was unable to say anything in that moment, Bruce nodded. Elizabeth then said, "Is it because you as well as your friends thought you all got rid of me for good after destroying my house completely to the ground?"

Bruce said in response, "Yes, we did think that. Why is it that you are still around instead of being forever gone from our lives?"

Elizabeth giggled for a moment and replied with, "Well, I think I already told you why that is if you already forget."

Bruce tried to remember what it was that Elizabeth had already told him of why she was still around. The moment he finally remembered Elizabeth's answer to why she was still around, Bruce said, "Because we might not have destroyed the house entirely."

Elizabeth smiled and said, "That is right, Bruce. Very good in remembering that."

Bruce then asked, "How is that possible? We all saw that house got destroyed, and nothing was left standing."

Elizabeth then said, "Let me ask you this: did all of you experience strange things inside the house only?"

Bruce thought about what Elizabeth had just asked him and said in response, "No, it wasn't. We were confronted by tree roots in the front of the house when we went back to the shuttle bus to leave Ben with Lora after he got really hurt, and then go back to the house to look for the others whereabouts."

Elizabeth continued with, "Well, now you should figure out what exactly does that mean."

Bruce responded with, "That we didn't get rid of you for good and that you are going to come back to start collecting souls of those who enter your house of infinite horror."

Then Elizabeth said, "And I know that I won't have to worry about you or any of your friends going back to my house to finish what all of you wanted to do at first."

Bruce then asked, "Why do you say that?"

Elizabeth replied with, "Because after what all of you went through in and outside my house, I doubt that your friends would want to go back to the place that may have given them an experience that would be hard to forget."

Bruce realized right away that Elizabeth might be right about his friends. After he realized that, Bruce asked, "And are you thinking I would be the only one to go back to your evil house?"

Elizabeth smiled and said, "Well, I do have my doubts about that, but I will make you go back to my house and see how you do in trying to destroy whatever you need to so you could finally get rid of me."

Bruce replied with, "And how are you going to make me go back to your cursed house?"

Elizabeth said in response, "By haunting your dreams until you do so and make you see what could have occurred if your friends didn't fight back when I possessed you."

Bruce was both shocked and surprised after what Elizabeth just told him. Then after he heard how Elizabeth was going to make him go back to her house, Bruce said, "If that is your plan in making me go to your house once again, then I will tell the others everything you have told me, especially your plan in having me return to your house alone since you think they won't ever go back to your house even if it was for my well-being."

Elizabeth nodded. "That is correct. Do you think I might be wrong about how your friends will respond when you ask them to go back to my house and tell them the reason why as well?"

Bruce answered with, "Yes, because if they still refuse after I give them the reason why, I will then tell them that you have planned to haunt me in my dreams until we or myself go back to your house."

Elizabeth smirked. "Well, good luck in doing that, because you already know what will happen until all of you or you alone go back to my house to finish what every single one of you wanted to do in the end, which was to get rid of me forever."

Bruce responded with, "No matter if I do this alone or with my friends, I will make sure that you actually are forever gone from all of our lives."

Chapter 20

After Elizabeth started to walk back outside the house and go into the darkness, she stopped midway and said, "Before I go, I would like to give you a little sample of what is to come to you in your dreams if you don't go back to my house by yourself or with all of your friends." A moment later, Elizabeth quickly flew toward him. She had turned into some kind of monster.

When she was in his face, Bruce woke up and repeatedly screamed no a few times. After he was awake, Bruce noticed he was sweating throughout his body. Then after he noticed that, Bruce got out of bed and went to the bathroom to clean the sweat off him. The moment Bruce was in the bathroom, he got a small towel that was meant to do just what he wanted.

When he got all the sweat off him, Bruce tried to calm himself and try to forget the nightmare he just had that involved Elizabeth as well as the threat she gave him. Bruce then told himself repeatedly that it was only a dream.

Then from out of nowhere, a voice said, "If you keep on telling yourself that, it just shows me how much the dream affected you, which makes me happy to know that very much."

Bruce immediately realized whom the voice belonged to. Then Bruce said, "You are not here or in my head, and I will have anyone or just myself to go back to your demented house!"

Elizabeth responded with, "Well then."

THE HAUNTED HOUSE

When Bruce turned around to see Elizabeth in the mirror, he was in complete fear as well as shock by that sight.

Elizabeth smiled and said, "Let's see how long you will keep on saying that until you give in or lose your mind." Suddenly, Elizabeth progressively turned to her true form, and it frightened Bruce so much he wasn't able to move or even speak. When she was finished turning into her true form, Elizabeth said, "I hope to see you or your friends come back to the house soon, and hope that your mental state is all right when you do."

After she told Bruce that, Elizabeth jumped toward Bruce. Everything went dark when she got into his face again.

The next day, Bruce woke up on the floor of the bathroom in a small puddle of his own sweat. A short while later, after he put a towel over the puddle of sweat and took another shower to get rid of the foul smell that he was giving out probably because of the sweat, Bruce tried to calm himself and not lose his mind, like Elizabeth wanted him to.

When he finished taking a shower, Bruce dried off with a towel and thought about what he should do next, because his state of mind was on the line. Bruce had to decide if he would go back to Elizabeth's house to finish destroying whatever he needed to destroy to get rid of Elizabeth for good by himself or with his friends.

A moment later, there was a knock on his door, and he asked, "Who is it?"

The response was, "It's us, Bruce. Could you let us in so we can talk for a bit?"

Bruce then said, "Just give me a minute to get some clothes on." When Bruce got some clothes on, he went to the door and let his friends in. After everyone was in his house, Bruce asked, "What is it that all of you want to talk about, because I also wanted to tell you all something that could be important for everyone to know."

Steve then said, "Well, let us tell you that Ben is all right now and will be recovering for a few months."

Marissa continued with, "And we were having trouble going to sleep last night for some time before we finally were able to sleep in peace." The moment Marissa told him that, Bruce replied with,

"Elizabeth visited me last night in my dreams." After he told the others that, they all had the expressions of shock and surprise on all their faces.

Then John asked, "Was it the real one? Because that can't be even possible after what we did to her house."

Sarah followed with, "Yeah, that's right. Elizabeth is supposed to gone from our lives for good after destroying her house completely to the ground."

Bruce said in response, "Elizabeth told me that we may have destroyed her house but we didn't everything that she owned."

Marissa then asked, "What else is there that we needed to destroy to actually get rid of Elizabeth once and for all?"

Bruce replied with, "The property grounds are what we needed to destroy to get rid of Elizabeth forever from our lives as far as she told me in the dream I had last night." After Bruce told the others that, they were all surprised with his response as well as confused by it too.

A moment later, John asked, "Did she tell you anything else last night?"

Bruce responded with, "That she is going to make my life difficult until I go back to her house by myself, or with any of you that would agree to come back with me, to try to destroy what we need to so we can do what we all tried to do the first time around."

Then after Bruce told the others that, they were shocked to find out Bruce was being forced to go back to Elizabeth's house by being tormented by her until he does. That moment, all of them knew what they wanted to do to help Bruce out in the situation he was in right now.

Steve said, "I think I speak for everyone when I say that we will go with you to help destroy Elizabeth's property."

Bruce looked at the others to see if what Steve told him was true. After he saw everyone was in agreement to go help him destroy Elizabeth's property, Bruce thanked everyone and asked them if it was a good idea to get Ben involved with destroying Elizabeth's property. John answered with, "I think we should wait until Ben is fully recovered from all of his injuries, don't you all agree?"

THE HAUNTED HOUSE

Bruce and the others thought about what John told them to see if he had a fact about them waiting after Ben has completely recovered from all his injuries to then ask him if would like to join them to destroy the property grounds of Elizabeth. A moment later, everyone realized they should wait until Ben has completely healed from his injuries to find out if he wanted to come with them to destroy Elizabeth's property so they can finally get rid of her for good.

Marissa then asked, "And what about Lora, should we ask her to join too?"

Bruce replied with, "I think she won't come with us if Ben doesn't come as well."

The others immediately realized that Bruce was telling them the truth about Lora staying if Ben did too. After they all knew that Lora's response would be the same as Ben's, Leslie asked, "So what should we do now?"

Bruce stood in the center of his living room and said, "Well, I think all of us should wait until Ben is fully recovered and find out what the answer is going to be to what we are going to ask him."

Steve followed with, "But that will be months. Don't you think that will be difficult for you, Bruce, to do since Elizabeth will be haunting your dreams until the day you go back to her house?"

Bruce said in response, "I know that, but I have to wait and see if Ben will join us, which will also tell us if Lora is coming as well."

Marissa then asked, "Even at the cost of your well-being, both mentally and physically?"

After a short moment, Bruce replied with, "I want to have at least all of the people that wanted to get rid of Elizabeth from our lives to finally actually do it no matter what the cost. Besides, I'm already in a way damaged mentally, so that just leaves whatever physical damage I will receive in the wait for Ben's full recovery."

After Bruce said to the others, John then asked, "What do you mean that you're already damaged mentally? How exactly is that?"

Bruce said in response, "I think all of you know how because I was not exactly myself or in control of the actions I did to you and Steve."

When the others heard that, they immediately realized what Bruce was referring to. Then Leslie asked, "How did that damage you mentally if you were not the one harming them but Elizabeth?"

Bruce replied with, "I know that, but she made me watch as she was hurting and then trying to kill Steve by strangling him to death."

Everyone was shocked when they heard that, for it might have been a moment that Bruce could never forget. Bruce continued with, "So no matter what happens to me physically, it can't be any worse than remembering that every day for the rest of my life."

After Bruce told the others that, John said, "Well, if that is the case, we will wait for Ben to fully recover to find out what his answer is going be, and each of us will check up on how you are doing every once in a while, if that is okay with you."

Bruce smiled and nodded.

A while later, back at the gas station, Mike and Bob were setting things up before closing the station for the rest of the day.

A moment later, Mike asked, "Are you sure we should close the gas station for the day? It's only twelve in the afternoon."

Bob answered with, "I got a call from the owner telling me to close the gas station for the day."

Mike followed with, "Did you ever ask him why he wanted us to do that in the middle of the day?"

Bob said in response, "Well, he found out that the other stations were having low income in customers the past few days, so he wanted to have them close for the remainder of the day, as well as go on a brief vacation until he calls us to go back to work."

After Bob told Mike that, Mike nodded, ask what he was going to do when they finished setting things in order before closing the station.

Bob replied with, "I was planning to go up the road to California and go to some of the interesting sites they have there instead of going home."

Mike thought about it for a moment and then said, "Do you mind if I come along with you?"

Bob asked why Mike would want to come along with him to California instead of going home.

THE HAUNTED HOUSE

Mike answered with, "Because I have never gone to California ever in my life, and I would like to go there with someone instead of going there alone."

Chapter 21

Bob thought about it and agreed to let Mike come along with him to California to see the many sites it has. A short while later, Bob and Mike finished putting in order all the things in the gas station as well as the auto shop.

Mike asked, "Do you think we could get some snacks for the trip?"

Bob said in response, "Yeah, I think we should bring some snacks with us on this trip, and we are in a place with the perfect selection of snacks to choose from, don't you agree?"

Mike looked around the station to see all the snacks they could choose from. After he saw them, Mike said, "Do we get the employee discount or not?"

Bob replied with, "We do get the discount, but it isn't much that it takes off the overall price." When Bob told him how much do they get as a discount, Mike thought about what they should take with the amount they get cut down on the final sales price. After he finally came up with a plan, Mike said, "We should get most of the cheap snacks and drinks."

Bob then asked, "Why do you want to do that?"

Mike responded with, "Well, since we are going to California to see all the sites it has, I thought we could save our money so we could use it to buy souvenirs at each of the sites we go to, as well as get gas when we need to."

THE HAUNTED HOUSE

When Bob realized what Mike had told him was a fantastic idea, they both went to get the cheapest snacks and drinks both of them wanted to take with them on the trip.

By the time both of them paid for their items, Mike followed Bob to his car. After they put their stuff in the back of his car, Bob and Mike set themselves in the front of the car, with Bob in the driver's seat. A moment later, Bob asked, "Are you ready to go, Mike? Because I am."

Mike nodded.

Bob then started the car and got on the road to California right away. When they were what both of them thought to be a mile away from the gas station, the front of the car suddenly began to puff a lot of smoke. Bob drove the car to the side of the road so he could check out what happened to the front of the car.

When he parked the car to the side of the road, Bob quickly got out and went to the front of the car. After he was in the front of the car, Bob said, "Mike, pull the lever to pop the hood." The moment Mike pulled the lever as he was told, Bob lifted the hood and checked to find out what happened to the engine that would cause it to suddenly fume a lot of smoke from out of nowhere.

A moment later, Bob finally found out what exactly happened to the car's engine. Bob then said, "Mike, we have a serious problem with the engine."

After Bob said that, Mike got out of the car and went to the front of the car where Bob was at. When Mike was finally at where Bob was at, he asked, "What exactly is the problem we are having with the engine for it to suddenly puff a cloud of smoke?"

Bob answered with, "As far as I can see, the engine seems to have been punctured somewhere underneath."

Mike then asked, "Are you trying to find out what exactly punctured the engine right now?"

Bob nodded. Mike followed with, "I can help you find it more quicker."

Bob said in response, "Sure, and you can help by going underneath the car's hood to find whatever it was that punctured the engine."

Then Mike asked, "Why do you think it might be under the car's hood?"

Bob answered with, "Because in case it is not anywhere I can see from where I'm currently looking at, it might turn out somewhere underneath the car, don't you think?"

Mike thought about what Bob told him to see if he was right to have him look underneath the car for whatever punctured the engine. He realized the engine was somehow pierced by an unusually big splinter, which was strange since the car started to break down while it was still on the road.

After he found the cause of the car breaking down, Mike tried to take the big splinter out of the car's engine. When Mike finally got the splinter out of the engine, he went to the passenger's window to show Bob the exact cause of the car to break down. Bob was surprised by the size of the splinter and then said, "What should we do next?"

Mike told Bob they could take the car back to the gas station and see if they could find out if the motor shop had the part of the engine that severely damaged by the splinter. A moment later, Bob thought of something and was about to tell Mike about what he came up with before it suddenly started to rain out of nowhere.

When it started to rain, they knew both of them had to come up with a new plan. A short while later, Bob saw something a few yards away from where they were at right now. Bob told Mike about it and asked him if he could make out what it was for he wasn't able to do so. Mike was able to make out what the thing was Bob had seen ahead on the road.

He told Bob to get out of the car and walk to it so they could get some shelter until the rain stopped. The ground around was wet as well, and it was difficult to move back to the gas station to repair the part of the engine that was damaged by the splinter. A short while later, they were in front of the thing both of them had seen from a distance.

Mike then said, "This place looks a bit spooky, but mostly looks very old and falling apart."

Bob asked, "Do you think anyone lives in this house?"

THE HAUNTED HOUSE

Mike responded with, "I don't know, but we could still stay in there until it stops raining and the ground around the car dries up enough to move it back to the gas station without any problems or complications."

Bob thought Mike had a point and agreed to see if anyone lived in the house. When they got to the front door, Bob knocked and waited to see if someone would respond. The moment no one responded, Mike was about to knock on the door before it suddenly opened for some reason.

Then a woman came out from the dark, with a lantern in her right hand while the other was on the door. The woman was wearing ragged clothes that appeared to be from the past. Both of them thought the clothes could be about one or two hundred years old, and the way the clothes seemed to look could be the main factor to that thought.

Mike then said, "Hi there, miss. We were wondering if you can allow us to stay in your house until the rain stops and the ground dries up."

She told them they could, and asked them for their names. Mike introduced Bob and himself to the lady but never told her their last names for his own reasons.

Then Bob asked, "Can you tell us what your name is, miss?"

The lady responded with, "My name is Elizabeth Griffin. Please come inside my house."

After they were both in Elizabeth's house, Bob said, "It is quite impressive that the inside of your house looks better than the outside."

Elizabeth replied with, "I know, but the outside looks like that because it recently got quite weak, but I'm going to get it refurbished as soon as possible."

A moment later, Mike noticed Elizabeth still had the front door open and was looking outside for some reason while they were looking around them. Mike then asked, "What are you doing, Elizabeth? Are you expecting someone?"

Elizabeth answered with, "I'm hoping that a relative of mine comes back soon, and hopefully brings his friends with him again too."

Bob said in response, "How long has it been since your relative came to your house with his friends?"

Elizabeth replied with, "It has been a while, but not too long since he and his friends last visited my house."

Then Mike asked, "Do you know if they are going to come back to your house anytime soon?"

Elizabeth responded with, "Well, I left him a message that I'm hoping it will convince him to come visit my house again, and he can invite his friends to come visit as well."

After Elizabeth told Bob and Mike that, she started to slowly shut the door. Before she was about to completely shut the door, Elizabeth said, "Even though I don't know when or if he is coming anytime soon, I am going to get the outside of the house into a better shape anyway."

Bob then asked, "Would you like us to help you out with that?"

Elizabeth smiled dementedly and said, "Don't worry, both of you are going to help with the outside of my house, but in a different way."

They were wondering what Elizabeth meant with that, but before either of them could ask her, Bob and Mike both noticed something happening to Elizabeth all of a sudden.

Elizabeth's appearance started to change before their eyes. Her appearance was drastically changing into something that had Bob and Mike frozen in place, and were both getting anxious as well as worried in what Elizabeth was turning into. A moment later, Elizabeth stopped changing, which meant she had completed her transformation that frightened Bob and Mike by what she turned into in the end.

They saw she had white hair, long nails, fangs, and black eyes with white pupils. While they were frozen in place and now wrapped in complete horror by Elizabeth's appearance, she then said, "I think it's about time I get to work refurbishing the outside of the house with the help from the two of you."

They couldn't move, because both of them were still in complete fear. They tried to scream but were only able to do so before they were silenced by Elizabeth.

THE HAUNTED HOUSE

After Elizabeth killed Bob and Mike in the house, Elizabeth started to somehow absorb their mauled bodies into the floor. This made something out of the ordinary occur to the outside of the house, as it suddenly began to progressively repair itself. Every part of the house that was damaged or severely out of shape on the outside was slowly getting into a better form as well as shape.

A short while later, the outside of the house was completely repaired as well as refurbished, and it made the outside look good as new. Elizabeth turned back to her usual form. When she was in front of a window and was able to see outside, Elizabeth smiled dementedly and said, "Come back to the house, Bruce. And bring all of your friends if you can so I can see if any of you can actually get rid of me, now that I have told you and you might have told your friends how to do so. But this time around, I won't go easy on any of them or show mercy to no one, except you. For you will be by my side, whether you want to do so or not."

END

About the Author

J. A. Garcia was born in Santa Ana, California, on December 19, 1991. He is the eldest son of a family of eight. He is the first man in his entire family to get a standard high school diploma. He has always been the kindest person to all his friends and family. J. A. Garcia started to write his stories in middle school in an English class. He did very well in writing assignments from middle school through high school. J. A. Garcia was an average student from elementary school to high school, and was in the special education program as well as English-language learners program. He has had some struggles with depression and anxiety in the past but is now doing better than he was before.

J. A. Garcia has been known to be a helpful person to his friends and family whenever they needed his help with something they were not able to complete and/or do by themselves. He has been told he has Asperger's and was the reason why he struggled to be at certain events like parties of any kind and be around a huge crowd of people he doesn't know. J. A. Garcia struggled in college, mostly because he was not part of the program that would be somewhat similar to the special education program he was in before. These days, J. A. Garcia has improved with his struggle with being unable to go to all kinds of parties and be around a large amount of people he doesn't know. This he finds to be quite the accomplishment for himself.

Printed by BoD™in Norderstedt, Germany